MW01118624

MIDSHIPMAN HENRY GALLANT IN SPACE

H. Peter Alesso

THE HENRY GALLANT SAGA

Midshipman Henry Gallant
at the Academy © 2022
Midshipman Henry Gallant in Space © 2013
Lieutenant Henry Gallant © 2014
Henry Gallant and the *Warrior* © 2015
Commander Gallant © 2016
Captain Henry Gallant © 2019
Commodore Henry Gallant © 2020
Henry Gallant and the Great Ship © 2020
Rear Admiral Henry Gallant © 2021

Other Novels

Captain Hawkins © 2016
Dark Genius © 2017
Youngblood © 2018

MIDSHIPMAN HENRY GALLANT IN SPACE

H. Peter Alesso

hpeteralesso.com

VSL Publications
Pleasanton, CA 94566

Edition 9.00
ISBN-13: 978-1482640328

∞

Not everyone who fights is a warrior.

A warrior knows what's worth fighting for.

United Planets—Jupiter Fleet
Captain Caine
6 Battlecruisers – Repulse, Renown, Remarkable, Retribution, Dauntless, Devastator
72 Eagle Fighters
72 Bombers
5 Destroyers
12 Auxiliary Support Ships

Marines on Ganymede
Colonel Ridgewood
7th Marine Regiment

Mars Fleet
Admiral Collingsworth
18 Battlecruisers *Superb*
48 Cruisers
96 Destroyers
72 Auxiliary Support Ships

Titan—Jupiter Fleet
6 Battlecruisers
24 Cruisers
144 Destroyers
144 Auxiliary Support Ships

Titan—Main Fleet
12 Battlecruisers
70 Cruisers
288 Destroyers
288 Auxiliary Support Ships
24 Orbiting Battle Stations
120 Ground Missile Bases

CONTENTS

JOINING THE FLEET

1

A massive solar flare roared across the sun, crackling every display console in the tiny spacecraft.

"No need to worry, young man. We're almost there," said the aged pilot.

"I'm not concerned about the storm," said newly commissioned Midshipman Henry Gallant. Eagerly, he shifted in his seat to get a better view of the massive battlecruiser *Repulse* that would be his home for the next two years. She was a magnificent fighting machine, a powerful beast in orbit around Jupiter.

The pilot maneuvered to minimize the effects of the x-ray and gamma radiation until the craft slid into the cold black shadow of the *Repulse*. Gallant could hardly contain his delight as the tiny ship quivered in the grip of the warship's tractors.

By the time the docking hatch finally slid open, Gallant was waiting impatiently for his first glimpse inside the warship.

He hurried to the bridge. The officer of the watch stood next to the empty captain's chair, surrounded by a dizzying array of displays and virtual readouts. The officer rested his hand on the panel that concealed the Artificial Intelligence (AI) tactical analyzer.

"Midshipman Henry Gallant, reporting aboard, sir." Drawing his gangly seventeen-year-old figure to its full height, he gave a snappy salute. He tugged at his uniform jacket to pull the buttons into proper alignment.

"Welcome aboard, Mr. Gallant. I'm Lieutenant Mather." Mather was of average height, barrel-chested with angular facial features and a stoic look. Beyond a glance, he showed little interest in the new arrival. "Give me your comm pin."

Gallant handed over his pin, Mather made several quick selections on a touch screen, then swiped it past the chip reader.

While his ID loaded into the ship's computer, Gallant took the opportunity to look around. The semicircular compartment, though spacious, bristled with displays, control panels, and analysis stations.

From his academy training, he could guess most of the functions. There were communications, radar, weapons, and astrogation, plus a few he couldn't identify. Several of the positions were vacant operating automatically. Gallant's fingers twitched, eager to be a part of the bridge's efficient operation. A huge view screen dominating the compartment displayed Jupiter. An orbiting space station was visible against the vastness of the gas giant. He marveled at the spectacle.

"Junior officer authorization verified. The ID pin has been updated with *Repulse's* access codes," a computer's voice announced from a nearby speaker. Its neutral, disinterested tone reminded Gallant of a rather cold and distant teacher he had had in basic math years ago.

"Did you bring your gear aboard?" asked Mather.

"My duffle bag is at the docking port, sir."

The aged pilot had helped Gallant carry his gear from the shuttlecraft onto *Repulse*. Then, after a cheery smile and a friendly, "Good luck," he climbed back in his shuttle and left. Having no family of his own, Gallant had found some faint comfort in the good wishes.

"I'll have your gear sent to your quarters. But, for now, you had better see the captain," said Mather, raising an eyebrow at Gallant.

"Aye aye, sir," said Gallant.

Mather turned to one of the bridge's junior officers, a young woman. She wore a single thin gold stripe on her blouse sleeve, indicating her rank as Midshipman First Class, one-year senior to Gallant. He ordered, "Midshipman Mitchel, take Mr. Gallant to the captain's cabin."

As they left the bridge, Mitchel said, "Henry Gallant . . . I remember you from the academy. I'm surprised you're still in uniform."

Gallant gritted his teeth, as he had done many times before when confronted with what he perceived as overt disapproval. He didn't recognize her, but he couldn't help but observe that she was an attractive brunette with a trim figure.

"Will you be training as a fighter pilot or missile weapons officer?" she asked.

"I had basic fighter training on Mars and will be taking advanced pilot training with *Repulse's* Squadron 111."

"I'm a qualified second-seat astrogator in 111. Most likely, we'll wind up flying together at some point."

Because her demeanor revealed nothing about whether that idea repelled or appealed to her, Gallant nodded.

When they reached the captain's cabin, she said, "I'm Kelsey, by the way." Then, as she turned to leave, she added as an afterthought, "Good luck."

Gallant watched her walk away. He wondered if her remark was sincere.

Gallant stood like a statue inside the open hatch.

Captain Kenneth Caine was seated with his back to him, reviewing Gallant's military record, which was displayed on a computer screen. Clean-shaven with close-cropped graying hair, Caine was solidly built with square shoulders and a craggy face. His well-tailored uniform hugged his robust frame, accentuating his military bearing.

From his brief time onboard, Gallant had already realized that *Repulse* was an orderly ship, and that Kenneth Caine was an orderly captain. Precision and discipline were expected. He was suddenly conscious that his tangled brown hair was longer than regulations allowed.

The cabin was sparsely furnished in a traditional, starkly military fashion. A desk in one well-lit corner held the single personal item in the room: a photo of an attractive, mature woman with a pleasant smile. The sadness in her eyes hinted at the difficult bargain she had made as the lonely wife of a dedicated space officer.

While the captain flipped through the personnel folder, Gallant's gaze wandered to the compartment's viewscreen. The solar flare had subsided, leaving gigantic colorful Jupiter filling most of the view.

"At ease, Mr. Gallant," said Caine, finally turning to face the newcomer. "Welcome aboard the *Repulse*."

Gallant relaxed his stance and said in a strong, clear voice, "Thank you, sir."

Caine looked him up and down and scrunched his face before asking, "What do you know of this ship's mission, Mr. Gallant?"

"As the flagship of the Jupiter

Fleet, *Repulse* must prevent alien encroachment along the frontier, sir," ventured Gallant.

"Quite right, as far as that goes. But you'll find, Mr. Gallant, that this task is more nuanced and layered than may be apparent. As a United Planets officer, you must find shades of meaning that can affect your performance. What would you surmise is behind this frontier watch?" The captain's brisk voice demanded a resolute answer.

Gallant spoke guardedly at first, but as his confidence grew, his voice gained assurance. "Well, sir, UP knows little about the aliens' origins or intentions. They appear to have bases on the satellites of the outer planets. Clashes with their scout ships have proven troublesome, and Fleet Command wants to gather more intelligence. With so little known about alien technology, it isn't easy to assess the best way to repel it. Still, this fleet must forestall an invasion of Earth by preventing the aliens from gaining a foothold in this sector."

"And what would you say will be essential in achieving victory in battle?"

Leaning forward with his hands behind him to balance out his jutting jaw, Gallant said with fierce intensity, "Surprise, sir! I assume that is why you've dispersed most of the fleet. So you can search the widest possible region of space for the first signs of significant alien activity."

Caine examined the young man again as if seeing him for the first time. "Good. *We* will not be the ones surprised. *We* will be prepared. You can appreciate how important it is that *Repulse* performs well." Then, he added, "And I will allow nothing, and *no one,* to interfere with our mission."

"Yes, sir," said Gallant, feeling the sting from the pointed comment.

"Tell me, Mr. Gallant," said the captain, shifting in his chair to find a more comfortable position, "why did you apply to the academy?"

Gallant's voice swelled with passion. "For as long as I can remember, I've wanted to pilot spaceships and explore the unknown, sir."

"You are undoubtedly aware that many people wanted your hide raised up the flagpole." Caine's eyebrow twitched. "Although your progress for two academic years at the academy was respectable, many doubt that a Natural can compete in the fleet. Today, your real qualification for advancement is your double helix."

Caine continued, "Frankly, I'm astonished you have gotten this far without the advantages of genetic engineering. You're a bit of a mystery that has yet to unfold."

Gallant didn't like being referred to as a mystery, but he had his own uncertainty about how his future might evolve.

Caine said, "Now that you are commissioned, you must serve a two-year deployment on *Repulse.* Then, if you complete all your qualifications and receive strong ranking marks, you may be recommended for promotion to ensign."

He gave a weak smile and added. "Learn your

duties, obey orders, and you will have nothing to fear."

Caine searched Gallant's face. "Well, nothing to say for yourself?"

Gallant thrust his chin out and said, "I am prepared to do my duty to the best of my ability, sir!"

"It is exactly 'the best of your ability' that is in question, young man," responded Caine.

THE BEST OF YOUR ABILITIES

2

The captain's parting words weighed on Gallant's mind as he stepped tentatively against the ship's artificial gravity.

The size of a small town, the *Repulse* bustled with activity. Fresh air hissed gently against his face as he passed the ventilation ducts. They replaced the stale, odor-laden air from the cramped compartments. Air conditioners droned steadily, fighting the heat buildup from the running equipment. Underneath it, he felt the heavy rumble of the oxygen generators and carbon dioxide scrubbers.

The corridor was well-lit with smoothly paneled bulkheads. Behind the paneling were piping with flowing fluids, ventilation ducts, and electrical conduits.

After a few twists and turns along the well-lit corridors, Gallant lost all sense of direction. He couldn't tell fore from aft, let alone find his way to the midshipmen's quarters.

Finally, he gave up and touched his comm pin to ask the computer for directions.

"Turn left ahead, take the next ladder down to deck four, and turn right to compartment 4-150-0-L," responded the disembodied voice. "The compartment number consists of four parts: deck number, frame number, centerline position, and compartment use, such as L for living space." Gallant wondered if the smugness he heard in the computer's tone was just his imagination.

The midshipmen's common room was roomy with a large central table. Along the starboard bulkhead were a dozen narrow two-person quarters for the men, with another dozen opposite for the women. Two doors at the far end led to common washrooms. Several desks jammed into the compartment's corners offered cramped study areas. At the head of the table was a large video screen, currently dark.

Various activities were apparent: studying, playing games against the computer, or each other. They murmured about the day's trivia as they performed their duties. The overall atmosphere seemed relaxed and pleasant until Gallant walked in. In the sudden silence, his eyes swept around the room.

The group consisted of first-class midshipmen, roughly split between men and women. Their insignia indicated a mix of pilots, astrogators, and missile officers.

"Does he speak, or must we use telepathy?" asked a redheaded giant at the foot of the table. His bodybuilder torso contrasted with his agreeable brow and mischievous grin. His deep booming voice could have come from a baritone singer.

"My name is Gallant."

"Well, Gallant, come closer and meet your brethren," said the redhead. "I'm George Gregory, better known as 'Red' for obvious reasons. This is Anton Neumann, notable for his manifold inherited talents, but especially for his pilot skills." Red gestured toward a young man standing at the head of the table, who had been reading studiously but now looked at Gallant with interest.

Neumann was, in every way, the prototype of Earth's most advanced genetic engineering. His hauntingly handsome face revealed a rare combination of beautiful symmetry and inner strength. And his tall robust frame exuded power.

His position at the head of the table confirmed him as the ranking midshipman.

"And that's Jerril Chui, who enjoys torturing musical instruments," Red continued, pointing to a tall, wispy figure with a drawn complexion. A lighthearted laugh twittered around the table.

"Tell us a little about yourself, Gallant," interjected Chui before Red could continue with more introductions.

"Well, there's not much to tell. This is my first

deployment. I'll be taking advanced fighter training," he said with increasing discomfort.

"What's your genetic quotient?" interrupted Neumann. Everyone waited quietly for Gallant's response. Such a direct request for a genetic quotation was considered impolite. If they'd been young businessmen at a social gathering, the question would have been rude to the point of insult. However, the directness of military discipline lent itself to candor.

"I am . . . unrated," responded Gallant, steeling himself for what he knew would follow. The effect he had on others was far too familiar: first, the reaction of his classmates at the academy and now here in the faces of his shipmates. Each pair of eyes shifted uncomfortably. Facial expressions changed from open and good-natured to guarded and reserved.

Neumann smiled benevolently. He opened his hands and turned them up as if to suggest, '*Look nothing up my sleeves,*' before he said, "I thought I recognized your name. You're the Natural?"

A man who could assume a benign appearance while injecting a disparaging accusation was not to be trusted. The duplicitous playacting aroused Gallant's suspicion and disappointment, for he knew what was to follow.

He grimaced as he replied, "Yes." He locked eyes with Neumann for a full minute. He felt a tingling of defensiveness as disappointment crept into his mind.

From that moment, Gallant's very existence seemed to evaporate from the consciousness of the other midshipmen. Instead, they simply went back to their previous activities, ignoring him.

A humiliating sense of rejection burned through Gallant as if he were on fire.

He noticed his duffle bag leaning against the last starboard cubicle. Shrugging, he walked to his new quarters and unpacked his few belongings.

Crawling into his bunk, he sighed a little at the sound of the others talking and laughing gaily into the night. Though he had started the day with high hopes, he wasn't surprised by his crewmate's reaction. A little prickle of anger made the hairs on his neck stand up.

There was, of course, no such thing as a superman—but there could be.

It used to be that natural selection ruled Earth. But dreams of superbeings lurked in the fantasies of children. They hoped that one day, supermen might arise through genetic engineering and deliver an aspirational Golden Age.

As the only Natural in the fleet, Gallant tossed sleeplessly in his bunk. He was uncertain of what awaited him, but he was determined to meet every challenge head-on.

As he finally nodded off in the early hours, his mind drifted.

Did Kelsey really wish me good luck?

AN EVEN CHANCE

3

I n the summer of 2166—when Gallant first reported to the Space Academy—the days were warm on the Mars equator.

The warmth came from over a century of terraforming. The release of carbon dioxide from the ice created greenhouse gases that warmed the planet as they built up in the atmosphere. Rivers flowed as the ice melted. Oxygen generators used the abundant minerals in the Martian soil to create a breathable atmosphere. With each passing day, Mars became home to a growing dynamic United Planets citizenry. To meet the daunting challenges, they worked and sacrificed most of the 687 days every year.

It was Gallant's first time on his own.

Looking across the academy yard from the main gate, he saw a tiny patch of lush green lawn. Its manicured shrubbery was a striking contrast to the imposing granite buildings and marble monuments.

Symbols of history, both ancient and recent, emphasized the hallowed nature of the institution. A few rare trees cast long shadows down the red brick walkway.

A cluster of new arrivals chattered excitedly on their way into the administration building. They greeted him cheerfully, made him feel welcome. The future might be uncertain, but for that wonderful moment, he relished the achievement of just getting into the academy.

Soon, he stood among his fellow classmates, taking the oath of office in the Space Force. He finally felt he belonged, despite his heritage. All he needed was an even chance to prove it.

At least that was how Gallant remembered it when the buzzing alarm jolted him awake.

He had slept fitfully on the coffin-sized bunkbed within his tiny cubicle quarters. He had the bottom bunk along the metal bulkhead. The cubicle also included two tiny storage lockers. One was for his clothes and personal belongings. The other, like its associated bed, was unoccupied.

He could hear others stirring outside, already on their way to the washroom.

A virtual computer display popped up over his bunk.

"Attention, Midshipman Gallant. You have fifteen minutes to complete your morning ablutions and dress. Then you are to report to the executive officer (XO) at 0600 hours in office 3-250-0-Q."

"Great," he said in exasperation as he jumped

out of bed, gasping when his feet hit the cold hard metal of the deck. Even before the computer's voice had faded away, he shuffled into his slippers and his hand reached for a towel. He dashed through the common room to the officer's showers.

The shower sprayed icy water over his body for the prescribed thirty-second allotment. He recoiled as the cold permeated his flesh. He shivered through the twenty-second antiseptic cleanse and a ten-second rinse.

Showered and shaved in four minutes, he took a few seconds to appraise his reflection in the mirror. It revealed a face of steely determination, but he couldn't deny the inexperience of youth that lingered there as well.

He donned his uniform and jogged to the XO's office, his comm pin chirping out a series of right and left turns as he navigated the corridors.

"Midshipman Henry Gallant, reporting as ordered, sir," he said when he reached the XO's open hatch.

A single word greeted him from within, "Enter."

Commander Eddington, *Repulse's* XO, sat engrossed with a virtual computer display. His office bulged with large and small pieces of equipment, most of them damaged. In one corner, more hardware poked out the top of unspoiled cartons. A few random uniforms were also strewn about the room. Either the XO's office substituted for a garage, or he was moonlighting as the ship's supply officer in his spare time.

His pallid, bloated face matched his oversized body. The ruffled hair and scraggy beard might have suggested a muddled mind, but Gallant suspected they were the product of a harried work schedule beset with frequent crises.

The XO looked up at the ship's chronometer and sighed. He was apparently occupied with some issue of significance, whether minor or major, it was hard to tell. Nevertheless, he put aside the problem to focus on Gallant.

He scanned through the computer information. "Gallant . . . classes . . . grades . . . mmm . . . flight training . . . fighter qualifications . . . fitness reports . . . harrumph."

The litany went on for several minutes while Gallant remained at attention, trying to keep his "eyes in the boat." He knew that letting his attention wander would draw a rebuke.

Finally, the XO sat back in his chair and picked up his coffee mug. Sipping at the hot brew, he gave Gallant an appraising look and asked, "How did you get assigned to *Repulse*? Did you request this duty assignment for your two-year space deployment?"

"No, sir. My three requested duty assignments were all for ships at Mars Station. I was told those positions were being filled by more qualified midshipmen, but that Jupiter Fleet had an opening for a replacement pilot. So, I sort of volunteered, sir."

The XO almost choked on his drink. He spat, "Volunteered, eh?"

"Yes, sir."

"Well, your primary duty here will be fighter pilot, but we've a great deal more to offer you, training-wise. Since you qualified on a basic fighter trainer on Mars, you'll first re-qualify on our Eagle fighters over the next three weeks."

The XO spoke very fast, "Eagles are two-seaters, so that's a change from the training craft you're used to. As a pilot, you will fly and handle weapons. Your astrogator will plot and feed you course and acceleration maneuvers. In addition, the astrogator will handle engine and environmental monitoring. Of course, you will have command of the craft and bear full responsibility for its performance."

The XO said, "Once you complete re-qual, you'll begin advanced flight instruction and prepare for your final flight exams in three months."

"Aye, aye, sir."

"Give me your comm pin. I'll code you into the wireless network for the ship's library. It includes operational, technical, and repair manuals. It also provides course instructions and exams."

Gallant gave him his pin.

"You will complete all the online instructions and simulations. You will take the AI-administered exams on the schedule the system lays out. That covers your flight training. Also, you will qualify as a duty officer on this ship within six months. Mmm . . ., let's see . . ." He paused and looked over the ship's roster. "We currently have enough Engineering Officers of the Watch (EOOW), so you will qualify as Officer of the Deck (OOD) first. That means standing watches as Junior Officer of the Deck (JOOD) until you qualify to conn the ship. You can complete your engineering training next year. Also, you will relieve Mr. Neumann as communication division officer within two days. I hope you remember something of your training from school. Your leading petty officer is Chief Howard. He's a good man. Let's hope he can keep you out of serious trouble."

"I uh ...," Gallant had a stunned look on his face.

"You got a problem with any of that?" asked the XO with a raised eyebrow.

Gallant set his jaw and furrowed his brow. "NO SIR! I'm going to do just fine . . . sir."

The XO managed a small smile and said, "Let's hope so."

Then he grinned, "Your additional collateral duties—to fill up your spare time—will be assigned later."

"Aye aye, sir," said Gallant, swallowing hard.

"That's all. You're dismissed."

Midshipman Neumann spent thirty minutes turning the communications division over to Gallant. He quickly ran through the classified documents, equipment, and personnel files. He demonstrated the procedure for taking incoming messages, decrypting, and distributing them. He explained how internal ship communications interfaced with the artificial intelligence computers. Then he took Gallant to the

Combat Information Center (CIC). There were radars, telescopes, communications, and data plots where the intelligence was analyzed.

"This is the division's leading petty officer, Chief Benjamin Howard. He'll introduce you to the sixteen men in the division and give you a tour of CIC and the division's spaces."

One look and Gallant could tell Howard was a seasoned veteran. His jaunty stride marked him as a man who had developed his 'sea-legs' navigating a varying gravity. His thinning brown-gray hair and a slight potbelly took nothing away from his immaculate uniform, well-creased trousers, and mirror glossed shoes. The cluster of decorations on his chest illustrated an eminent career.

"I'm glad to meet you, Chief."

"Pleased to meet you, sir."

Impatiently, Neumann offered his tablet for an electronic signature. It described the turnover status of critical elements of responsibility within the division.

As Gallant began scanning it, his gaze locked on the final column. His heart gave a jolt. It showed a perfect one-hundred percent operational readiness, with zero outstanding deficiencies.

He looked directly into Neumann's deadpan gray eyes. He knew what he should do—must do. He took a deep breath . . . but let the critical moment pass without challenging Neumann's status report. Instead, he signed the tablet and returned it for countersignature.

Neumann signed and turned away, marching rather than walking out of the compartment without further comment.

"Would you like a tour now, sir?" Howard asked with a pleasant smile.

"Yes, please."

They strolled through the CIC together, squinting under the glaring lights of the brain center of the battlecruiser.

Howard pointed, "Over there is the sensing equipment, including active radars and telescopes. On this side of the compartment is astrophysics and plotting which compute the course and velocity of contacts. Every object we track has a specific emission signature that we can identify. The spectrum of our emissions is strictly controlled."

Howard waved, "Over here is the communication array. The information is critical for command and control. One of our most covert communication devices is this burst transmitter. It emits a focused beam only the recipient can detect. We handle priority and action messages. The ultimate responsibility for carrying out action orders is the captain's, of course, but he knows who to go to if any messages are lost or garbled."

"Speaking of responsibility" commented Gallant. "The turnover report showed classified messages with zero deficiencies."

"That's completely accurate. Our equipment can detect, decrypt, and translate every letter of a message even at minimal signal strength. Our encryption and decoding equipment are the best, and we are meticulous in documenting our work."

"The unclassified monitored message traffic was also marked one hundred percent with no defects. Can you tell me how that is possible?"

"Even the best equipment has limitations. For unclassified monitoring of routine communication, we can keep almost perfect records."

"Almost, but not one-hundred percent?"

"Well, if the signal is logged out before it has faded to the degradation level, we don't have to account for it as lost information."

"And Neumann made that standard practice for the division?"

Howard shrugged.

"What about that decryption equipment that those two men are working on. The turnover sheet showed one hundred percent of equipment operational with no deficiencies."

Howard dropped his smile. "Hagman and Curtis are repairing the main long-distance transmitter. That's one of the things you should have asked Mr. Neumann about before signing the turnover."

"True, but I'm asking you now."

Howard's face contorted.

"Could you give me the unofficial version, Chief?" Gallant realized he was asking for a leap of faith; he hadn't yet earned.

To his credit, Howard revealed, "Well, according to the captain's standing orders, equipment malfunctions must be reported no later than noon every day. Mr. Neumann's orders were that we did not report any equipment out of service *until* noon. Instead, he required us to drop everything and repair any faulty equipment immediately. That kept everything showing in service on the central status report."

"But that means others wouldn't know they couldn't depend on that equipment being available."

Howard looked troubled but didn't add anything.

"What about maintenance? Is everything perfectly on schedule with no deficiencies there too?"

"There are demands throughout the ship. If equipment goes down for maintenance, it interferes with operations. Mr. Neumann took advantage of a thirty-day grace period for exceeding maintenance due dates if parts have been ordered. He believed in ordering plenty of spares, even if we had some on hand."

"How much of the equipment is behind their maintenance schedule, unofficially, of course?"

"Eleven percent."

"Wow," Gallant gasped.

"It's your division now, Mr. Gallant. What are your orders?" asked Howard, taking the measure of his new boss.

Gallant reflected for a few seconds and then said, "Any equipment out of service will be reported to CIC, immediately. It will remain out of service until it is fully tested and back on-line."

A smile returned to Howard's lips. It was

obvious to Gallant that the man loved what he did.

"Also, you and I will work out a maintenance plan that will get us back on schedule as soon as possible, despite the inconvenience to normal operations."

Chief Howard looked at Gallant with a sympathetic eye. "If you're feeling a little overwhelmed just now, let me assure you, sir," his grin widened ear to ear, "it'll get worse."

Gallant hoped he wouldn't regret his decision. He said, "I'd appreciate any help you can give me, Chief."

Howard said, "I'd be glad to help in any way I can."

"Thank you, Chief. I appreciate that."

"Okay. Let's get started, and I'll show you how to keep things running without losing any action messages. That, at least, will keep the captain from shooting you right off the bat."

Gallant knew he was going to like Chief Howard.

***

By the end of the first week, Gallant was again standing in the XO's office.

Commander Eddington thundered, "What are you doing with the communications division, Gallant? In one week, you've logged more equipment out of service for repairs and maintenance than Mr. Neumann did in the six months he was division leader. And what's up with the garbled messages? We never had that trouble before. Are you letting Chief

Howard do his job?"

The XO's admonishment worried him, but Gallant held firm. "We're conducting necessary maintenance and repairs, sir."

Eddington's red face deepened another shade. "I want you to live and breathe maintenance and repair until everything is back to peak efficiency, just like you found it. If not, I will have you relieved, and your record will reflect this failure. Is that clear enough for you?"

Gallant kept his own counsel. "Yes, sir."

On alternate days, Gallant attended basic flight training classes under Lieutenant Mather.

Mather reviewed some of the fundamentals for the class. He said, "Flying in an atmosphere is a matter of aerodynamic fluid flow to propel a jet and change direction. The jet engine thrusts the craft forward, ailerons guide airflow in the direction you wish to steer, and flaps create friction to slow the craft."

He watched the heads nod. "There is no fluid flow to redirect when you are flying in the vacuum of space. Instead, we use Newton's second law, action-and-reaction. The main engine thrusts the ship forward, bow and side thrusters direct high-energy plasma in the direction we don't want to go. Fire bow thrusters to slow, right thruster to go left, and so on. It's all a matter of pure power. Apply enough directed thrust, and you can maneuver radically."

There were a few puzzled faces.

"Do you have any questions? Remember, there are no dumb questions, so go ahead and ask," said Mather.

On student ventured, "Sir, I get that there is a difference between aircraft and spacecraft, but I don't understand how to use thrusters because there is no gravity in space."

Mather laughed. "Okay, maybe I was a little optimistic about there being no dumb questions. Of course, there is gravity in space. You are confusing weightlessness with the absence of gravity. Weightlessness occurs when gravity and acceleration are balanced, like in a fast-dropping elevator. For a moment, you feel weightless, but it's just because your weight balances against the acceleration of the drop in height. You are still in a gravity well. Gravity is present throughout the universe and only varies by the distance to nearby mass. Any other questions?"

The F-715 Eagle was a sleek, elegant fighter with twin anti-matter engines for lightning acceleration. Gallant smiled the moment he laid eyes on it. It included an anti-missile missile (Mongoose) designed for defense against incoming anti-ship missiles. In addition, it had a 1.21 GigaWatt (GW) pulsed laser cannon.

Compared to the high-powered Eagle, the clunky, single-seat nuclear trainer he had flown on Mars was a dog. He began to appreciate that requalifying as a fighter pilot on this ship would be a real challenge.

The pilot and astrogator sat in tandem, with the pilot in the forward seat. The cockpit had enough room—barely—for the crew to stand and maneuver. In addition, a small bunk bed was crammed in a crawl space below the crew's seats for rest during extended flights.

Midshipman Sandy Barrington was assigned as Gallant's re-qual flight instructor. Thin and nervous, with exaggerated lines around her mouth, this young woman took life very seriously. She was an expert pilot and was intent on demonstrating the Eagle's capabilities. She allowed him to get the feel of flying the fighter under her guidance.

"Okay, Gallant, move into position for catapult launch," she ordered.

Gallant slowly maneuvered the craft across the hangar deck to the guide slot for the starboard catapult. It was possible to launch using only Eagle's engines, but that was allowed only during battle conditions. The exhaust heat scorched the bay area and required extensive cleanup.

During his short flights around *Repulse,* she lectured him on technique and demonstrated the ship's capabilities. When not otherwise occupied, Gallant spent several hours every day in training sessions.

Work clobbered Gallant. He spent every available minute with Howard and Hagman, working on getting equipment back up to spec with minimal downtime. He helped read the repair manuals while the men worked to replace circuits or modify the software.

Slowly, the CIC status board reflected improvement. Meanwhile, Gallant was falling behind his AI scheduled assignments and the simulation exams.

Despite his best efforts, Barrington was relentlessly critical of his performance. She piled on simulation assignments to supplement his actual flight time.

Over the next few days, Gallant found his division work melding with his re-qual study and training simulations. Soon everything blended into a blur of constant activity. His occasional brushes with other midshipmen were strictly professional and impersonal.

Late one night after a grueling flight training session, he literally walked into Kelsey Mitchel when he stumbled around a corner. His bloodshot eyes widened.

"Oh, sorry, I wasn't looking . . . I was thinking about . . . ahhhh . . .," he stammered. Then with a final, "Sorry," he bounded away before she could say anything.

Nearly two weeks after his last visit, Gallant was once again in the XO's office.

"Gallant, I don't know what I'm going to do

with you. You're behind in your re-qual assignments, and you failed your last two simulation exams. I'm marking you deficient in your studies. Your final re-qual exam is tomorrow. Fail that, and you'll be sent packing back to Mars. This is your last chance."

SEEING STARS

4

In the weeks since Gallant reported aboard Repulse, his days overflowed. He had fighter qualification, duty officer training, and division officer obligations. He was grateful that Chief Howard had more than once saved an important message from going astray.

Late that night, he dragged himself to the midshipmen's common room for some much-needed qualification study time. But the area was already occupied with busy midshipmen, so he made his way to the wardroom. Officers were permitted to do their work there when meals were not being served. He peeked in and saw that the room was empty. He flopped into a chair and put his feet on the adjacent one.

With his Eagle qualification looming, he wanted to work on some practice questions before turning in for the night. So, first, he ran through a series of drills on his study tablet. Then he activated the tablet's flight simulator and practiced accident recovery maneuvers.

When Mather entered the wardroom, he nodded at Gallant and punched his authorization code into the galley panel.

The auto-server popped up, displaying a tray of synthetic bars, a few pieces of natural fruit, and a small portion of nuts. Mather picked at the nuts and fruit, leaving the synthetics for last.

Deep-space ships always carried plenty of synthetic materials that could be turned into edible food. The trouble was that human appetites yearned for the real thing. So, space stations stockpiled real food for the fleet. But in Jupiter's orbit, the cost of transporting bulk food materials so far from Earth was prohibitive.

Gallant's stomach growled, but snacks were not a midshipman's privilege. And though he would have liked some exam advice, he knew better than to ask.

Mather sat absent-mindedly for several minutes, tapping the edge of the table as he finished the last snack.

Finally, he said, "I've reviewed your training status with the XO. You've finished your classwork and written exams. It's time for your qualification flight. Are you ready to take your test in the morning?"

Startled, Gallant bolted upright in his chair.

"In the morning?" he asked as his voice broke. Despite his preparations, he didn't feel ready. Finally, his mouth went dry, and his eyes opened wide.

Suddenly, the idea of taking the qualification exam was the worst thing he could imagine.

Who would be following my performance?

Not only the captain and officers but the entire crew.

If I fail to qualify, I'll have to face them all. They'll know that without genetic engineering, I'm inadequate. Just what they expected.

He swallowed hard.

I'd rather postpone the exam and keep them guessing.

Mather stood up in front of him, waiting for a response.

Gallant lowered his gaze and bit his lip. "I need more time."

Mather scowled. His eyes stared right through Gallant.

He said, "You've had the normal allotment of time. You should be ready, but I'll tell the captain you've confessed that you're unprepared. He will decide if you can take a few more days. Is that what you want?"

Mather leaned closer, hovering over Gallant.

Gallant blinked.

If I don't at least try, everyone will consider me a coward. It's better to get it done. If I'm not up to their standards, I might as well know now than later.

He looked up at Mather. "No, sir. I'm ready to take the exam in the morning."

Mather's face relaxed. "Good. I'll make the arrangements for 0600. You'd better get to bed. You're going to need a good night's sleep."

Mather left the wardroom. Gallant got up to head to his quarters but stopped as the XO entered.

Gallant froze as Commander Eddington snapped, "Where are your personnel fitness reports? They're late. I want them first thing in the morning."

Before Gallant could respond, the XO strode off to deal with another of his endless litany of problems.

"All part of the job," Gallant said to himself with a sigh and sat back down.

He popped several stim-pills for an energy boost and pulled up the fitness reports for his division's personnel on his tablet. He relied on Chief Howard's draft notes for guidance. He spent enough time on the evaluations and rankings to feel comfortable with the final grades. After a couple of hours, he was still only half-finished.

Leaning back in his chair to stretch, he considered putting the files away and snatching a few hours of sleep before his re-qual flight.

Eddington hadn't sounded very accommodating.

With another sigh, Gallant rubbed the sleep out of his eyes and returned to work on the personnel records. He dropped them in the XO's cyber in-basket before the morning watch changed.

Then he trudged to his quarters and laid on his bunk. It was 0500. He closed his eyes and waited for the morning alert.

At 0545, a virtual computer display popped up over his head and blared, "Attention, Midshipman

Gallant. You have fifteen minutes to complete your morning ablutions and dress. Then, report to Squadron 111 hangar at 0600 hours to take your requalification flight exam."

The usual morning mad dash began. Standing before the bathroom mirror, he smirked at his sullen reflection.

He said, "Buck up, Kiddo, this will be a rough ride."

When he reached the flight deck, the captain was already waiting. Both Commander Eddington and Anton Neumann were standing beside him.

The XO said, "Captain, Gallant has passed all simulation training and written exams."

"Excellent," said Captain Caine, looking pleased. "Are you ready for your final flight test, Mr. Gallant?"

"Yes, Captain," said Gallant with as much earnest zeal as he could muster.

"I assume the XO has explained the process. You will proceed from Jupiter Station, circumnavigate Jupiter, and return to the *Repulse*. A flight monitor will take the Eagle's second seat in the place of your astrogator. He will not assist you in any way."

Caine narrowed his eyes as he searched Gallant's face.

Gallant remained expressionless.

"You are to handle all navigation and engineering duties yourself. The flight monitor will initiate computer simulation failures into your ship's AI. Although the accidents will not harm the equipment, the AI will lock them until the flight monitor reinstates them. For example, if one of your twin engines is marked as damaged, you will fly on one engine. If your environmental system is tagged as inoperable, you must ration the air supply until you return. A complete menu of system failures and accidents is available to the flight monitor. He will decide which problems you will encounter at his discretion."

Once more, Caine paused. Then, finally, he asked, "Any questions?"

"No, sir." Gallant knew that that was the only acceptable response.

Caine said, "Mr. Neumann has volunteered to be your flight monitor."

Gallant winced. He thought this might not end well.

Caine turned to Neumann. "At all times, you are ultimately responsible for the safety of the spacecraft. If, for any reason, Mr. Gallant fails to respond correctly to the accident scenario, you will terminate the exam. You will then take over the spacecraft and return to the *Repulse*. Are you ready, Mr. Neumann?"

"Yes, sir."

"Very well, gentlemen. Proceed to the hangar. You have permission to begin your flight exam."

Minutes later, with Neumann in the second seat behind him, Gallant pulled on his neural interface gear and took off.

He maneuvered the Eagle away from the ship. A fighter could circumnavigate Jupiter in an hour at maximum acceleration. Considering simulated accidents and system failures, the flight would undoubtedly take longer. Under Neumann's supervision, Gallant expected his test to last most of the day.

For thirty minutes, the Eagle flew flawlessly. When they reached, the far side of Jupiter, alarms and warning lights erupted from every corner of the cockpit. Gallant interpreted the emergency indications through his neural interface. He formed a mental image of the casualty and evaluated the information data feeds.

The AI reported, "Fires in port and starboard engines—control panel and main electrical panel fused—atmospheric supplies contaminated—antimatter plasma containment field ruptured . . ." the computer droned on, listing other system failures as they registered.

He threw the kitchen sink at me.

Neumann had entered a dynamic series of

system failures orchestrated by an AI computer virus. It worked to sabotage his systems as soon as he restored them. It was a cunning ruse. Not explicitly against the exam rules at first glance, but a severe review would be necessary if he filed a complaint. Gallant was stuck. If he couldn't overcome this disruptive AI from stopping him from every simple repair, he wouldn't qualify.

Without hesitation, Gallant cut the engines. He shut down the environmental equipment and pulled the plug on the internal cockpit power. He initiated fire suppression systems and crawled into his armored spacesuit, noting that Neumann was already in his.

Neumann had red-tagged so much equipment that Gallant hardly knew where to start. He drew resolve from the knowledge that once he got a grip on the problems and repaired them, Neumann wouldn't be able to do much more to him.

"Give up?" asked Neumann, wearing his broadest smirk.

"No."

"Why not? You will fail."

"Can't you let me complete the test?"

"You can't."

"Why don't you at least let me try?"

"Because," said Neumann, color rising in his cheeks, "I know that when it counts, you'll let us down. Face it; humanity has moved on. You're a relic."

"Have you ever considered the possibility that you might be wrong? Maybe one of the downsides of genetic engineering is that it eliminates advantageous random mutations. As a result, humanity could miss the next branch of evolution."

"And that's supposed to be someone like you? You're full of yourself. Besides, the idea is ridiculous. By eliminating weaknesses and reinforcing strengths, genetic engineering guarantees superior development. You need to accept that."

There it was. The emotional slap in the face, the blind bigotry of the genetically engineered. For a second, Gallant hung his head to avert his eyes at the shame he felt. Then as quickly, he decided he wasn't going to bow to Neumann.

He looked up, eyes blazing. "I'm going to prove you wrong!"

Without another word, Gallant gave his full attention to analyzing the signals.

He toiled in vain.

After the first hour, Gallant was lost in a maze of data and information that wouldn't conform to anything sensible. In addition, the AI virus was blocking his moves and making active countermoves.

The second hour passed in total confusion. Again, he was frustrated as secondary systems failed. Only this time, it wasn't Neumann's doing. It was a result of the errors he made.

The Eagle was like a musical instrument out of tune, playing a sour song.

In the third hour, Gallant felt as if he should quit and save himself from further embarrassment.

Damn. I know this stuff. Why can't I figure this

out?

Finally, Gallant decided if Neumann wasn't going to play fair, neither would he. He turned off every running system. Then he disabled the backups. Next, he pulled the plug on the emergency backup power.

The ship was now completely dead. It was an inert hunk of metal in cold space without power or life support. They would be dead in an hour.

"You maniac! What have you done?" screamed Neumann. He would have taken control and terminated the exercise, but there was nothing working to control.

Without answering, Gallant opened the deck panel to the ship's undercarriage and crawled into the equipment bay. He spent the next hour manually rebooting the emergency power and computer systems. Finally, he purged the AI virus command and began rebuilding the ship's functioning systems.

It was brutally cold in the cockpit, and Gallant could scarcely use his fingers to manipulate the switches and levers. Nevertheless, he could see his exhaled breath.

No. That would slow him down.

Without communications to complain to the *Repulse*, Neumann was left fuming.

By the fourth hour, Neumann blurted out, "We're stranded here; it's time for you to concede failure. Only those with the best genetic bloodlines should be officers. You don't have the ability. This complex AI interfacing is beyond you."

Gallant ignored him.

He almost got the engine restarted.

"Come on. Come on," he whispered.

He tried to coax life into the system.

"Please," he muttered.

Another hour passed, but each effort led to failure. It all collapsed again.

He looked at Neumann, who smiled triumphantly.

Gallant took a deep breath, shook his head, and started again.

After eight hours, Gallant's Eagle was still drifting around Jupiter as he worked to overcome the system failures.

Neumann grunted, "Give up. I'm tired. I want to return to the ship."

Gallant ignored him.

Then a single signal emerged and rose above the static.

A pulse. At last, everything made sense. He could see the mathematics in a symphony of harmony. As he figured out the failure modes for each piece of equipment, he submitted his solution to the ship's clean AI for evaluation.

At first, it rejected nearly everything he proposed. Eventually, Gallant restored the ship's life support and established minimal power.

Neumann's frown reinforced his determination to succeed.

He moved his fingers over the computer keys like a pianist. He watched as the dancing signals on the oscilloscope mingled with the electromagnetic fields.

He could hear the synchronization of the engines. They whispered at first, then grew into a roar.

Ten hours after the start of the test, he tried to restart an engine.

Neumann was ready for him. He initiated a new failure that knocked out his restored power—a nearly fatal complication. The ship lost life support again.

Gallant sucked in a breath. He knew that if he didn't satisfactorily resolve this problem, Neumann would be justified in failing him. To better concentrate, he closed his eyes and focused his mind. He visualized the ship, its controls, and the system failures as one integrated image. With a clearer picture, he then turned his senses toward finding a path to recovery. Developing a sense of harmony between controls and performance, he created a solution in his mind's eye. Despite his exhaustion, he finally submitted his repair concept to the AI. It approved the plan and ruled that both life-support and the minimal power supply were successfully restored.

After eighteen hours, Gallant had one engine operating at twenty-five percent power. It was enough to continue the flight around Jupiter.

Setting the autopilot and without stopping to rest, he kept working. He soon restored other systems, including radar and communications. Finally, they crept toward the *Repulse*.

A full twenty-four hours after leaving the

Repulse, Gallant's Eagle finally landed back in the hangar. By then, nearly every *Repulse* crew member had entered the ship's pool, betting on whether Gallant or Neumann would be flying the fighter.

Chief Howard made a killing when a faint voice crackled over the radio, thick with static, "Gallant to *Repulse* . . . –quest . . . permiss– to dock. . ." A cheer went up from the communications division.

"Who's flying?" asked Caine.

With a big grin creasing his face, Howard told the captain.

A few minutes later, a smiling Caine pinned the advanced fighter designation—a silver star—on Gallant's collar. It stood next to his thin silver midshipman bar.

Caine shook Gallant's hand. "Congratulations, Mr. Gallant. You're a starfighter."

FAUX WAR

5

A week after requalifying, Gallant attended an advanced training session. Even though his daily routine was a mixture of watches, reports, and examinations that interfered with his quest for food and sleep, he was eager to learn more.

Lieutenant Mather began his lecture by reviewing the ship's computer systems.

"Officers, the strong-AI system is nicknamed GridScape. It's a marvel of twenty-second-century technology." He pressed a panel, and a three-dimensional humanoid holograph appeared next to me.

Sandy Barrington stood up and asked, "What happens when there's battle damage, sir?"

"If the strong-AI system is damaged, we can switch to manual."

Neumann stood and asked, "How independent is the AI, sir?"

"The goal of creating independent, intelligent computers remains elusive. We have systems that can understand human language, solve problems, and navigate through space. But we can't fully rely on intelligent robotics. People will always argue about whether computers think. Our AI units think in a limited fashion, but they can only function within their prescribed range. In my opinion, the contest is which will advance faster—the future development of AI, or advances in our genetic engineering."

Looking at Gallant, he said, "Genetic engineering combines the best of your parents' DNA while removing harmful genes. It means that we no longer must fear inherited diseases. In addition, it activates helpful genes that promote neural stimulation. Success may come more easily for the genetically enhanced, but that's uncertain because the laws of chance still produce accidents."

Mather returned to his topic, "Once a target is designated, the AI can control *Repulse's* lasers and missiles. Our squadron of a dozen fighters will fly independently for close-in support. Today, we will conduct mock fighter combat to illustrate this point."

Mather paused for a moment, scanning the room. "Officers, you will be divided into teams—a blue team defending *Repulse* from an attacking red team. Please note that during the exercise, your fighter may register simulated battle damage."

Captain Caine slipped quietly into the back of the compartment and sat down while Mather continued with the assignments. Pilots Gallant and

Gregory were paired off as the blue team against the red team pilots, Neumann and Chui. Gallant and Neumann were selected as team leaders, and the designated combat area was set, along with a time limit.

Gallant's stomach flip-flopped between confidence and anxiety.

As the midshipmen boarded their two-person fighters, Kelsey Mitchel appeared next to Gallant. "I've been assigned as your astrogator," she said, her face and voice impassive. She went through the preflight checks professionally, hardly acknowledging him. He couldn't decide if her presence made him more nervous or less.

One by one, the Eagle fighters launched and took their starting positions.

Gallant pulled on his neural interface headgear and closed his eyes for a moment, concentrating. Dozens of silicon probes touched his skin at key points, picking up the wave patterns of his thoughts and processing them through the onboard AI. The AI translated his ideas into commands for flying the Eagle. The manual stick and physical control buttons in the cockpit served as a backup but thought control was faster and more accurate.

Gallant's eyes flew open as he *felt* a new world open to his awareness. In a flash, he could visualize the ship controls and equipment, as well as radar and optical scans that reached beyond his craft. As he oriented himself, his mind probed the controls for his fighter's propulsion and weapons. He could move the ship by visualizing what direction he wished to go. In addition, within a specific range of *Repulse,* he could interface with GridScape. He could even sense the emotional state of both Kelsey, in the astrogator seat behind him, and his teammate Gregory in the fighter next to him. He felt relaxed confidence coming from both.

Genetically enhanced midshipmen like Neumann used the neural interface seamlessly. It was more difficult for Gallant. In exercises on Mars, he had successfully interfaced with the neural headgear but wasn't able to maintain it for long periods. He would have to choose his moments of maximum effort carefully. He would rely on tactics that offered a brief respite from the intense concentration.

Gallant gazed through the Eagle's canopy at the void before him. He felt a sense of peace but remained ready for the coming challenge.

When Mather signaled for the exercise to begin, Gallant's first command was to accelerate the blue team away from both *Repulse* and the red team. Gallant hoped to give his team a tactical advantage by climbing higher in Jupiter's gravity well.

The physics of space battles were far different from what he had imagined when he first began training. The three-dimensional nature of space combat was fundamentally different from air combat. In principle, your enemy could come at you from any direction. But, in practice, spaceships were governed by orbital dynamics—not just by their ship's orbit around planets and suns—but by those planets' orbits.

Gallant could sense Gregory's uncertainty about his strategy, but he was sure Neumann would fall for his gambit. By drawing the red team away from its primary target, he hoped to gain a superior maneuvering position. It would give *Repulse* time to move out of the designated combat area. On the other hand, the extra distance meant he couldn't coordinate fire support from *Repulse* through GridScape. And if the blue team was knocked out of action, Neumann would have an unobstructed chance to attack *Repulse.*

His plan was risky.

As he anticipated, Neumann let his ego cloud his judgment, and he led the red team in pursuit instead of attacking the exposed *Repulse.*

Gallant smiled. A few minutes later, he reversed the blue team's course and dove into the pursuers.

The Eagle's bulbous midsection had a spinning rotor and a motorized gimbal that allowed dramatic changes in angular momentum. This control moment gyroscope (CMG) generated enough torque to let his spacecraft flip end-for-end in seconds. However, he watched as the antimatter gauge dipped noticeably from the rapid fuel consumption. As he accelerated toward the red team, he concentrated his team's firepower on the enemy's propulsion systems. As a result, the red team sustained considerable simulated damage.

His plan was paying off.

Gallant felt a surge of excitement. Then, he said, "Blue team, bank hard to port. Concentrate fire on the lead fighter."

Gregory mimicked Gallant's maneuvers as the two swung back toward their opposition.

But Neumann maneuvered his ship to avoid the worst of the laser blasts and scored numerous counterblows. As a result, Gallant suddenly found himself in a slugging match with opponents who were outstanding pilots.

In the ensuing dogfight, Neumann and Chui consistently outflew the blue team. Gregory tried to cover Gallant, but the simulated damage to Gallant's fighter mounted until the AI designated it destroyed. Gregory's fighter limped out of range, crippled but intact.

With Gallant and Gregory out of commission, the red team headed for *Repulse,* which was dashing for the safety of the combat area boundary. As time expired, *Repulse* fled the combat area with only minor damage.

The loss of Gallant's fighter tipped the scales to a victory for the red team.

With both teams back on the flight deck for the simulation review and debriefing, Captain Caine's only comment was a dry, "Most surprising, Mr. Gallant."

When Kelsey walked in for dinner, Gallant was slumped in his seat in the officer's mess. Then, to his surprise, she flashed him a luminescent smile and sat beside him.

She asked, "What's the matter? You look like death warmed over."

Tired from his mental exertions and deflated by the exercise's outcome, he replied, "Nothing."

"Something's bothering you."

Gallant shrugged.

"You're not brooding about the exercise, are you?" Her eyes conveyed a mature understanding.

Gallant grimaced.

"You're too sensitive."

"What? We lost."

"Get over it. You did fine. It was your first exercise, and Mather threw you in the deep end as the team leader. Neumann and Chui are a year senior to you, and they've also run that exercise a dozen times already. The fact that you kept us from getting slaughtered in the opening salvo was better than anyone anticipated."

"You included?"

Kelsey shrugged and began eating, occasionally commenting about the ship or its personnel.

Stirring his simulated coffee clockwise, Gallant watched with fascination as the liquid swirled in his cup. Then, finally, he stole a glance at Kelsey.

"Where is your family from?" he asked.

"Oregon, old-USA. We've been farmers for generations. My brothers help run the farm. Though with all the automation and advanced bioengineering, the only real variable is the weather. And even that's closely regulated, with the weather monitoring and seeding satellites. It's amazing how much food is produced from well-managed land these days. My family is proud to help feed people."

She smiled, studying the morsel of food on her fork. Then as if to illustrate how rapidly a hungry population consumes food, she gulped it down.

He reflected on the economic forces that drove the unified governments of Earth. Once colonization and asteroid mining began, commerce between the planets quickly followed. Eventually, immigrants in the planetary colonies sought full rights as citizens. Many people on Earth felt they had subsidized the colonies and should be repaid before citizenship was granted. In contrast, the colonists felt they had sacrificed much in facing deprivation and danger and deserved citizenship. After a short, sharp conflict, Earth and the colonies merged into the United Planets. They had a democratic government with a president and a congress. It granted the colonies equal citizenship rights with Earthers.

"I'm the first off-Earther in my family. We had some distant relatives who were early settlers on Mars but didn't participate in any revolutionary movements. Now they live just like everyone else —citizens of the United Planets," said Kelsey. She swallowed another bite and added, "Where are your people?"

"My parents died in an accident on Mars when I was very young," said Gallant, his face growing dark. "My grandmother raised me. She passed away last year while I was at the academy." For a moment, he saw his grandmother bending over him to kiss him goodnight. "I don't know about other relatives, on Earth or anywhere else. So, I guess that leaves me without any real roots."

They sat eating their meal quietly for several minutes.

Gallant finally said, groping for common ground, "I started training on an old fission-fragment rocket. They're designed to harness hot nuclear fission products for thrust instead of using a separate fluid as a working mass. The new antimatter engines dwarf that performance, of course. But the old rockets made good trainers. I learned a lot."

Kelsey said, "The antimatter engines are way

more powerful and responsive. The only drawback is that the fuel supply is still so hard to store in quantity."

After another moment of silence, she asked, "You love it, don't you? Space flight, I mean."

"I love the feeling of independence and self-reliance. It makes life an adventure. Usually, it's tranquil, but it can turn terrifying in a hurry," he said.

"I know what you mean," she replied. "But it sounds like you've found a home—in space."

Gallant nodded. "Why did you join up?"

"Someone needs to stand guard on the frontier. Everyone back home depends on us. I just knew it was the right thing for me."

"So, you're a patriot?" asked Gallant with a grin.

"Yeah," She looked at him and wrinkled her nose. "Right back atcha."

THE PENALTY
OF FAILURE

6

Gallant crawled through the ductwork between the ship's bulkhead and outer titanium hull until he reached the pneumatic-hydraulic plasma discharge valve for the starboard antimatter engines. Sweat and grease smeared his face and hands. His breath crystallized and released a misty cloud of cold breath as he wriggled through the tangle of cables and pipes. Finally, he cast his flashlight beam onto the automatic control setting and ensured it was closed. The green status light verified that the automatic closure feature was operating normally. He sighed with satisfaction and wiggled out of the duct and back into the corridor. This step completed his JOOD walkthrough.

The pre-watch walkthrough had taken Gallant

nearly twenty minutes. A visual inspection of all the ship's main spaces and any unusual activities was part of the process. In addition, it was required that each on-coming watch section confirm the automatic reports from the ship's AI computers.

Gallant wiped his forehead, picked his tablet off the deck, and tapped the last item on the watch stander's checklist.

Chief Howard said, "That's the hardest valve to verify, but we can't operate safely without it."

Gallant said, "I would have crawled along that duct forever if you hadn't told me exactly where to find it. Thanks."

Howard chuckled. "It's a favorite stumbling block on officer's training checkoffs. I've had some young go-getters lost for hours looking for it."

"I appreciate the hands-on tour."

"That's what they pay me for."

"While I'm at it," Gallant added, "Thanks for the help with the division records."

"They're nearly up to date now," said Howard. "I'll have Petty Officer Hagman finish them by next week's inspection." Then he yawned, "My watch cycle is done. I'm heading to chiefs' quarters to check my eyelids for leaks."

Gallant smiled as he watched the chief saunter away. Then he refocused his attention on the watch as he turned toward the engineering spaces.

He went through engineering spaces and checked in with the EOOW to check on any unusual conditions or repairs of interest during the watch. At the CIC he got their latest updates and quickly perused and initialed the CO's standing orders.

When Gallant reached the bridge, he reviewed the status display console, which showed the ship's course and contacts. Next, he tapped the screen to pull up communication and radar updates.

It was 2355 hours when he reported to the on-duty JOOD, Midshipman Neumann. Neumann had completed his engineering qualification during his first year on *Repulse*. Now, he was working toward his Deck qualification, just like Gallant. Neumann gave him a look of disdain as if waiting for him to make a mistake.

"I am ready to relieve you, sir," said Gallant.

"I am ready to be relieved," replied Neumann. "The captain has retired to his cabin. We're orbiting Jupiter, standard velocity and distance, no contacts, no special orders. One minor repair operation just getting underway in the forward missile compartment."

"Oh, I didn't see that repair team. Maybe I should walk through that space before—"

"I said it was a minor repair. It's correctly isolated from normal operations, and GridScape is monitoring it. No need for you to make a project out of it. It'll be completed before you can break a sweat."

Gallant took a deep breath, eyeing Neumann, and said with resignation, "Very well, I relieve you, sir."

"I stand relieved," said Neumann. He raised his voice to include the bridge personnel. "Mr. Gallant is the junior officer of the deck."

Five minutes later, Lieutenant Mather relieved the OOD, and he and Gallant began their six-hour watch cycle. As JOOD, Gallant sought every training opportunity each watch had to offer, despite Lieutenant Mather's lack of enthusiasm.

Repulse weighed 160,000 tons and had a length of 660 meters and a beam of 110 meters. Its armament included eight bow missile tubes, four aft missile tubes, ten short-range plasma weapons, forty laser guns amidships, armor belts, and force shields with electronic warfare decoys and sensors. The 2,814 officers and crew members were highly trained and used to dealing with the unexpected.

During the next hour, Gallant accomplished several minor housekeeping tasks. He called back to the engineering spaces to discuss an errant reading with the EOOW. A little later, he adjusted the ship's minimal shield strength to optimize power consumption. It still maintained adequate protection against meteorites. He examined the radar contacts and identified merchant ships transiting near Jupiter's moons. He also scanned through messages from the Ganymede Research Laboratory for unusual activity.

Jupiter Station was in orbit around Ganymede, just as Ganymede orbited Jupiter. The space station was a city with a population of over thirty-two thousand residents. It had served as a support base for the settlements on Jupiter's moons and the nearby asteroid miners for over fifty years. The facility had twenty main docking ports that could accommodate ships as large as a battlecruiser or cargo vessel. There were also hundreds of minor docking ports for smaller craft. The ports provided repair, maintenance, and refueling for both military ships and commercial ships owned by the NNR shipping company. NNR was the most powerful conglomerate in the solar system.

The station had defensive laser and missile batteries and a complement of Marines. In addition, a dozen small pioneer settlements on nearby moons were home to tens of thousands of colonists. The total population of Jupiter Station and the moons was around 352,000.

Although monitoring routine ship activities kept Gallant busy, his main interest was qualifying to maneuver the *Repulse*. Unfortunately, with the ship in a Jupiter orbit, keeping pace with Ganymede, no maneuvering was required.

Gallant was mindful that driving the *Repulse* through space differed from flying an Eagle. A fighter pilot used his neural interface to maintain intimate contact with the sensors and controls of his craft. His thoughts controlled the reactors and engines. *Repulse* was far too big and complex to be handled by a neural interface. He thought that might change one day.

Driving *Repulse* required the captain to set all the operating parameters. These included the ship's orientation, the effect of gravity wells in the vicinity, and then analyzing the strategic and tactical needs. Verbal orders were given to the helmsman, who manually entered input into GridScape. To reach the desired course and acceleration, the AI handled the details of adjusting the nozzle flow rate, fuel temperature, and thruster directions. While GridScape operated at the speed of light, it required much human direction.

The monotony of the watch was shattered at 0411 hours.

CLANG! CLANG! CLANG!

Mather said, "GridScape, report!"

"A fire is in the forward missile compartment," blared the AI voice.

Mather broadcast over the ship-wide intercom, "Attention all hands! Fire in the forward missile compartment! Forward Damage Control party, proceed immediately to the casualty."

He turned to Gallant. "Mr. Gallant, take charge of the DC party. Report to me as soon as you get there."

"Aye, aye, sir."

As Gallant bounded out, he nearly ran into Captain Caine, who stumbled onto the bridge, still buttoning his jacket.

Gallant threw himself toward each hatch until he reached the forward missile compartment. Clustered around the emergency supply cabinet, the DC team was scrambling into their protective clothing and breathing gear. Several members were already priming the fire suppressant apparatus.

Chief Howard said, "Mr. Gallant, DC team one is assembled, all accounted for. Fire extinguishing equipment at the ready. Two watch standers escaped from the compartment, but two repair team members are unaccounted for. They are presumed overcome by smoke near the source of the fire. Ready for ingress —we require access override codes to enter a volatile compartment."

Howard looked expectantly at Gallant and whispered, "You need to don protective gear, sir."

"Oh, right," said Gallant. He grabbed a set of protective coveralls and a breathing apparatus. As he put them on, he ordered, "GridScape open forward missile compartment hatch number 11289-B. Security safety lock override code Alpha-Alpha-19-Omega, authorization Midshipman Gallant, DC Team Leader."

The elliptically shaped hatch was five feet high and three-foot-wide and rose off the deck six inches. Its bulky reinforced alloy-steel frame had a wheel handle in the center and a bar latch across it. An access keypad and video view portal were just above the wheel handle.

GridScape blared, "Hatch unlocked and opened for ingress of DC party. The hatch will be immediately resealed. Future override can only be authorized by the captain. Acknowledge."

"Acknowledged."

The hatch retracted the mechanical latching mechanism and swung open.

The siren continued to blare as smoke billowed out. Gallant shoved one leg and then the other into his coveralls and stuck his head inside the hatch. Despite the spray from the overhead fire suppressant system, flames raged across several electrical panels.

Gallant's eyes stung from the fumes. He coughed as the acidic smoke burned his throat and lungs.

His adrenalin pumping, he said, "Follow me," and stepped over the lip of the hatch into the compartment. Struggling to get his arms through the coverall sleeves, he dropped both his gloves and the breathing mouthpiece. The next man was already stepping through the hatch, so rather than stopping to look for the gear in the dense smoke, he kept going.

The fire probably started where the repairmen were working.

He didn't know where that was but plunged forward, worried that the repairmen were probably unconscious. His mind raced, calculating the odds and options. Without oxygen, they would not survive long, and adding more fire suppressants would only make it more difficult for them to breathe. So, his only real choice was to find the missing crewmen before it was too late.

He stumbled forward several steps, all the while gasping. "Here, take a gulp," said Howard pulling out his breathing apparatus mouthpiece and stuffing it into Gallant's mouth.

Gallant took a deep breath and swallowed the bitter tasting bile that rose to his mouth. The welcoming breath helped him get his bearings. As his head cleared, he said, "Thanks," and plunged forward into the opaque compartment.

It took a minute for Howard to find a

replacement mouthpiece for himself, and then he began dispersing the DC team to fight the fire.

Everyone thinks I'll fail, thought Gallant. Everyone is wrong.

His eyes blinked against the stinging smoke, and his hands convulsed in pain from the heat. Swiping his arms back and forth to clear the smoke, he strained to see. After several tentative steps in one direction, he no longer felt the intense heat, so he backtracked and tried again.

Five feet . . . ten feet . . . fifteen feet . . . He saw an intense blaze by one of the refueling stations and shuffled toward it. He guessed some chemicals from the missile refueling station had spilled. A single spark from the nearby electrical source could have ignited the fuel.

Hoping Howard could hear him. He shouted, "Kill all the electrical panels on the port side. Shut down the isolation valves for the missile chemical refueling piping."

Gallant moved toward the refueling station, feeling the heat of the flames even through his protective suit. As he staggered forward, he tripped and nearly fell over the two repairmen. Another spasm of coughing racked his lungs, but he grabbed the men by their shirts and dragged them away from the flames.

After a dozen torturous steps, he felt willing hands from the DC team help him haul the injured men back to the entrance hatch.

Howard returned to the hatch and said, "The

fire is out. We need to ventilate the compartment."

Between coughing fits, Gallant tapped his comm pin and said, "Captain, the fire is extinguished. Emergency ventilation of the forward missile compartment is required. I request the compartment hatch be opened momentarily to permit evacuation of injured personnel."

Eyes widening, Howard said, "You better get your hands looked at, sir. Those burns look bad."

Gallant looked at the skin already peeling off his raw, blistered hands. Then, as a wave of pain washed over him, he doubled over and crumpled to the deck. Cradling his hands to his chest, he gasped for air like a drowning man, desperate to take a real breath.

A board of inquiry convened in the wardroom the next day.

The captain sat at the head of the long table. He was flanked by his senior officers— the XO, Commander Eddington; ship's engineer, Commander Sanchez; the science officer, Commander Jackson; the navigator, Lieutenant Commander Marshal; the operations officer, Lieutenant Mather; and the weapons officer, Lieutenant Stahl. They wore uniformly grim faces.

As the primary witness, Chief Howard, looking uncomfortable, was seated on the left side of the table. Midshipman Neumann sat next to him.

Midshipman Gallant stood at the foot of the

table, his heavily bandaged hands at his side. Eyebrows drawn down, he bit his lip and swallowed hard.

All eyes fixed on Gallant.

Captain Caine began, "The fire was started by a short in a faulty electro-pneumatic switch on the missile refueling tank. Fumes quickly overcame the workmen, but they were not responsible for the fire. The automatic fire suppressant systems were of limited value because the electrical panels were not isolated or shut down quickly enough. Efforts to control the fire were hampered by the high heat and a large volume of smoke in the space. Two repairmen suffered smoke inhalation, and three DC team members sustained minor injuries. All have been treated and released."

Captain Caine paused; his eyes boring into Gallant. "Mr. Gallant, why did it take you so long to isolate the source of the fire?"

"I had trouble locating the worksite, sir."

"Didn't you review the worksite on your pre-watch walkthrough?"

"No, sir."

"Why not?"

Gallant hesitated for a split second. "I didn't do a walkthrough of that area, sir."

"Why didn't you perform a walkthrough of that area before assuming the watch?" demanded Caine.

"No excuse, sir."

"There certainly isn't," said Caine, his neck flushing bright red.

Neumann shifted slightly in his seat but remained silent.

Caine continued, "Also, you failed to don protective gear and breathing apparatus before entering a smoke-filled compartment. That violation of the procedure may have contributed to the delay. It contributed to your smoke inhalation and burned hands." Caine paused again before asking, "How are they?"

"I'm okay, really, sir. Just a little tender for a few days, that's all," said Gallant, trying not to wince.

Next, the panel questioned Chief Howard to get his version of events. When they were satisfied, Gallant was excused. Finally, Captain Caine conferred with the XO and the department heads.

When they reconvened an hour later, Gallant resumed his stance at the foot of the table.

With a solemn face, Captain Caine said, "Mr. Gallant, for failure to perform an adequate pre-watch walkthrough and for procedure violations as DC leader, you will receive a letter of reprimand. In addition, you will undergo additional fire and damage control training."

"Aye aye, sir."

"But, off the record, good job dragging both repairmen to safety. They are expected to make a full recovery," said Caine.

GIANT EYE

7

Gallant shifted his weight from foot to foot as he stood beside the airlock to the Repulse's hangar bay. He felt conspicuous in his Service Dress Blues, but that was the required uniform for travel. Inside the hangar, a few crewmen and several passengers milled about, waiting to board the shuttlecraft to Jupiter Station. Eventually, his turn came, and Gallant took a long breath as he stepped through the airlock.

"Hello, young man. Remember me, Jacob Bernstein? Jake?" called the pilot, waving a hand.

"Yes, Jake." Gallant felt relief as if he had found an old friend. It was the same pilot who had brought him out to *Repulse* nearly six weeks earlier.

"It's good to see you. Come up front and sit next to me. You'll get a birds-eye view of the Great Red Spot, or as I like to call it, Jupiter's Eye," said Jake. "I hope you're doing well on your new ship."

"Yes. Everything is fine, thank you," said Gallant, edging forward out of the way of the dozen or so other passengers.

"Oh? What happened to your hands?" asked Jake.

"There was a fire. I was careless." Gallant sat down in the co-pilot's seat with a rueful grin.

"Tsk, tsk. You young men are all the same," Jake said, shaking his head. "So foolish. I expected better from you."

Gallant's smile broadened. "I'm fine. *Repulse's* doctors took great care of me. They dressed the burns, gave me some antibiotics, and sent my stem cell samples to the Jupiter Station hospital. That's where I'm headed, so they can graft the new skin over the burns. After that, it's no big deal. I'll be back onboard this evening. My hands will be just fine."

"Think before you act, young man, or next time you might lose more than a piece of your hide," Jake scolded.

"You're right. I'll be more careful in the future," said Gallant, patting Jake's arm.

Glancing back to the main compartment, Jake saw that most passengers were in their seats. With a wink at Gallant, he announced, "Ladies and gentlemen, please fasten your seatbelts. We will be departing in a few minutes," and shut the cockpit hatch.

When *Repulse's* hangar duty officer gave him clearance to depart, Jake started the shuttle's thrusters. He maneuvered the tiny vehicle out of the hangar and into the void, heading toward Jupiter Station in orbit around Ganymede.

"How've you been, Jake?" asked Gallant when Jake set the autopilot and leaned back in his seat.

"Oh, I can't complain. Well, I guess I could, but it wouldn't do any good," he chuckled.

"Why? What's the problem?"

Jake gave a short laugh. "Money," he said, "the cost of antimatter. You'd think with the Ganymede accelerator finally up and running, prices would fall. But it doesn't always work that way in commerce—not when the military has first call on the stuff."

"Do you own this shuttle business?"

"Yes, more than thirty years now. My family was among the first Jupiter frontier pioneers," said the old man with pride. "They came to the Kendra settlement on Ganymede as silicate miners. Later they helped develop a space habitat for colonizing the asteroids and moons. Did you know that asteroid fields vary in density? Mostly there's just space with a few rocks scattered around, but clusters of asteroids can block radar signals in some areas."

Gallant nodded and asked, "You've lived your whole life in Jupiter's orbit?"

"That's right. Plenty of folks live their whole lives in space settlements these days. You're probably used to Earthers, who take one space trip in their lifetime and think it's a great adventure."

"I've never been to Earth."

Jake said, "I grew up in the colonies but didn't fancy the mining trade. So, when I was old enough,

I started my own business. My dad supplied the down payment and secured a loan to get the shuttle. He also helped negotiate the military contracts so I could travel between military ships and the station. Unfortunately, my folks passed away, but I'm still at it. My wife, Margret, and I have a home on the station."

"Is she your only family?"

"Oh, no. My oldest son, Brandon, is a sergeant in the Seventh Marine regiment stationed near Kendra. My other three boys and their families visit from the Ganymede settlements whenever possible."

Gallant said, "My grandparents were pioneers too, settled in New Annapolis, Mars. My father was a terraforming engineer, and my mom was a mineralogist. They worked together and treasured everything about Mars. Those were magic years for us." He looked out into space, his expression darkening as painful memories crowded out the pleasant ones. "One assignment resulted in us being posted to an encampment on Phobos."

Gallant took a deep breath and wrapped his arms around his chest. "A large meteorite got past the laser defenses and struck our shelter." His eyes welled up. "My parents had only seconds to react. They sealed me in an escape pod," his voice wavered, "but they never made it to their own."

He sat quietly, staring straight ahead at nothing.

"I'm sorry, Henry," said Jake. He put his hand on Gallant's shoulder. "That's a harsh burden."

They were silent for a few minutes. Then to

change the mood, Gallant said, "Tell me more about your business."

"Well, let's see. It used to be quite lucrative. I operated under a military contract. They paid a base rate, plus a fee for each trip to ferry personnel and small cargo loads between ships and the station. At first, they paid for maintenance, repairs, and my flight time, even fuel was included in the contract. Now I pay my fuel costs. Oh, they upped some ferry prices, but not enough to cover the expense. Ganymede has an accelerator to produce antiprotons."

"The cost of antiprotons fluctuates because the availability depends on how much the military uses, right?"

"You got it. You'll have to excuse me now. We're approaching the station," said Jake. Then, switching the ship back to manual, he flew toward the docking port.

Jupiter Station's hangar bay was dark, dank, and dreary. Overhead air-conditioning vents emitted a frosty stream of vapor, stale from shuttlecraft exhaust.

Gallant shivered and pulled his jacket tight around him, shoving his bandaged hands into his pockets. His eyes were watery, and his nose was running from the chill. He sneezed, thinking about a steaming cup of stim-coffee, and was pleased to find he still had over an hour before his medical appointment.

Plenty of time for a cup at the Officer's Club.

After a short walk along the station's main corridor, Gallant opened a door into an elongated oak-paneled room with small tables cluttered with military paraphernalia. The crowded but well-lit room overflowed with cheerful banter, dissipating the gloom of the hangar bay. Bustling waiters moved about, serving the tables.

Gallant tried to edge past a short, plump man in elegant civilian attire. "Please excuse me, sir," he said, unsure of the man's rank or station. The stocky man nodded a vague acknowledgment but returned to his conversation without moving. Gallant squeezed by him and scanned the room for an empty table when he heard a familiar voice.

"Henry! Henry, over here!"

Craning his neck, Gallant saw Ed Stevenson weaving through the crowd of officers, trying to avoid knocking drinks over. As tall as Gallant and with sixty more pounds of brawn and sinew, Gallant's roommate had been a linebacker on the academy football team and was as tough as they come.

"Henry, it's great to see you," said Stevenson, arms extended in welcome. The bear hug almost crushed Gallant's ribs.

"Great to see you too, Ed," said Gallant, rubbing his chest, overjoyed at running into his friend. Just then, several officers vacated a nearby table. Gallant grabbed Ed's arm and pulled him toward it. They just beat out another young officer, who scowled as they plopped down into the seats, laughing and moving glasses out of their way. A waiter appeared to collect the empty glasses, wipe off the tabletop, and take their order.

"How've you been?" asked Gallant.

"I'm fine, but I'm stuck on Jupiter Station until *Renown* returns," said Stevenson.

"You're a missile weapons officer. I thought you rated immediate transport to your battlecruiser," said Gallant.

"Captain Rook left word for transient crew members to wait on the station," Stevenson said with a frown. Newly commissioned midshipmen were always eager to reach their ships because their two-year deployment didn't start until they reported aboard.

"That's unfortunate. I don't suppose there's any way to learn when *Renown* will be back," said Gallant. Stevenson shrugged and glanced at Gallant's hands. "What's with the bandages?"

"There was an accident on *Repulse*, a fire in the forward missile compartment. I was the DC leader, and I was careless. The burns aren't terrible. I'm due for medical treatment in about an hour," said Gallant. He hesitated, debating whether to tell Stevenson about the letter of reprimand.

"Well, until then, tell me about your ship. What's deployment like?"

"*Repulse* is a fine ship with a well-trained crew. Captain Caine seems strict but fair. I'm the communications officer. I suspect you'll get that same job in *Renown.* We haven't done all that much; beyond a few training exercises, we've stayed in Jupiter orbit."

Stevenson shot Gallant a sharp look. "Have you made any friends?"

Gallant managed a weak smile. "You know perfectly well; I'm getting the same silent treatment I got at the academy."

"Don't get discouraged. You worked through it at the academy, and you'll deal with it on *Repulse.*"

A new swarm of officers entered the packed room and tried to force their way to the bar. The ripple effect jostled the two midshipmen as the waiter handed them their drinks.

Gallant took a welcome sip before returning his attention to his friend. He said, "It took two years to make just a few friends at the academy. But, if it weren't for you and Sam, I would never have survived. You were both ideal roommates and wonderful to me."

"Who are you kidding? You didn't need any help from Sam or me. Nothing was going to stop you. Nothing did then, and nothing will now."

"Thanks, Ed. You don't know what a shot in the arm your support is," said Gallant. "Do you know how Sam is doing?"

"Wellman's an astrogator on *Superb,* the flagship of the Mars Fleet. I got a message from him a week ago, and he's doing fine."

"And how about you?" asked Gallant.

"I've been spending most of my time on AI training courses and availing myself of the local restaurants and taverns. Jupiter Station has some fun entertainment spots. I've met some nice local girls." He winked. "I can introduce you. Just say the word."

Gallant blushed. "Thanks, Ed, but there's someone on *Repulse* I kind of have my eye on."

"OK, I understand," laughed his friend.

They chatted for nearly an hour until Gallant reluctantly said he had to go.

"Can we get together again?" asked Stevenson.

"Count on it," said Gallant.

Outside the Officer's Club, Gallant tapped his comm pin to get directions to the medical facilities. Then, discovering it was farther than he thought, he called a taxi to take him to the hospital.

When he arrived, he signed in and waited until a nurse led him to a procedure room and told him to take off his uniform shirt. After removing his bandages, she put his hands on the surgical table and placed a sterile cover over each, exposing the burns.

"A little stick," she said, and he felt the needle's prick as she injected the analgesic.

"You won't feel any pain. You can watch, so long as you keep your hands perfectly still while the surgeon performs the procedure. Okay?"

Gallant nodded as the doctor entered and began looking over the wounds. Then, with his hands numbed, he watched as the surgeon peeled away the damaged skin, then grafted on collagen and the new skin grown from his stem cells.

While the nurse bandaged the repairs, the doctor smiled. "A perfect job if I do say so myself. If you had had genetic enhancements, your stem cells would have produced a cleaner match."

"Do you mostly see genetically enhanced personnel?" asked Gallant.

"Well, that's a complicated question. All fleet officers are enhanced because they use neural interfaces, either as pilots, astrogators, or missile officers. And sometimes even for general AI operations aboard ship. Hmm ... I see from your records that you're the single exception to that rule." The doctor paused and examined Gallant. "On the other hand, I also treat enlisted personnel, station workers, miners, merchant fleet personnel, and colonists. They are a mixed bag of genetically engineered and Naturals. As you're undoubtedly aware, although genetic engineering has been pretty much a routine Earther procedure for several generations, colonists have been slower to adopt the practice. I'm not sure whether the pioneer spirit of individuality motivates them or just a lack of adequate medical facilities in the colonies."

"Are the genetic enhancements pretty much the same for all people?" asked Gallant.

"Oh, no," said the doctor. "Everyone's DNA is unique, except for twins, of course. So, each DNA enhancement is a custom job. First, the doctor takes the DNA from the father—the sperm donor—and fertilizes an egg from his female partner. The DNA of the resulting embryo is then extracted and chemically altered by removing diseased or disadvantaged genes. Then favorable enzyme and hormone production genes are turned on. The fertilized embryo is then implanted in the mother's womb, and she carries the baby to term. The results are often good, but not perfectly uniform, hence the variation in performance of officers."

The doctor looked puzzled. "I don't quite understand how you can use the neural interface without the enhanced enzyme and hormone production. So, tell me, Mr. Gallant, how has your performance as a pilot been?"

"Adequate, doctor," said Gallant, shifting uncomfortably in his chair. Then, he asked abruptly, "What about my hands? When can I get the bandages removed?"

"You can remove the bandages in three days. You should have virtually no scarring. The results will be invisible to the eye."

ROOMMATE

8

Gallant sat on his bunk frowning at his touch-screen tablet, trying to coax himself into studying his latest GridScape training assignment. But unfortunately, the illustration of a complex system casualty was proving tiresome to evaluate.

A booming baritone voice destroyed his concentration. "Heads up!"

Midshipman George Gregory burst into the tiny room, his arms overflowing with uniforms and personal items. Then, after unceremoniously dumping his burden on the upper bunk, he asked, "Henry, how about giving me a hand?"

Stunned, Gallant sat frozen, looking back and forth between the nearly empty common room and the bear-sized intruder.

Finally, Gregory said, "The XO has assigned you as my wingman in Flight 4. So, how about a helping hand?"

"You're going to room with me?" asked Gallant, surprised at the good-natured twinkle in Red's eyes.

"That's the best way to develop teamwork. And from now on, we're a team . . . unless I'm not welcome?" asked Gregory, waiting for a response from Gallant.

In a flash, Gallant realized that far from the prejudice he assumed midshipmen held against him, here was someone who might be a friend, "Oh, you're welcome. But uhh . . . wouldn't you be more comfortable on the bottom bunk?"

"Now you're thinking, Henry! That would be great. And call me Red" He thrust his hand out.

Gallant shook Red's hand enthusiastically, "I'd be proud to, Red." The clothing was quickly hung in his locker or neatly folded in drawers. The shoes lined up on the locker floor. Red hung an image viewer full of pictures on the inside of his locker door. The image changed automatically every few seconds. Gallant caught a glimpse of family photos and a string of good-looking girls.

"Thanks for the help, Henry," said Red when they were done.

"Uh . . ., sure, glad to . . ."

"How about a game of chess?"

"That would be great," said Gallant, surprised at the invitation. This was the first since he'd arrived on the ship. He put his study tablet aside, vowing to make up the time after his next watch.

They went into the nearly empty common

room and began setting up the virtual four-dimensional space-time chess set. The few midshipmen in the room glanced at them and then returned to their business.

Behind his back, Red hid a white piece in one massive hand and a black piece in the other. When he brought his hands forward, Gallant picked the left hand, and Red opened it to reveal the white pawn.

Gallant began with a Queen's Gambit. Red wisely declined the gambit. As they played, several high-ranking pieces crowded the center of the multidimensional board, creating a heavier effective mass that stretched the board's virtual fabric. The effect limited the movement of these pieces. The bishops could only move a few squares along the diagonal.

Gallant concentrated, trying to make a good impression, but it was clear early on that Red was a master. Nevertheless, one of Gallant's moves caught Red off guard, and for several minutes he looked worried. Then, when he found a countermove, he laughed and slapped Gallant on the back.

"You almost got me there, buddy. Good job."

After that, Red dominated the rest of the game.

"Red, were those family pictures in your locker?"

"Yes. They show my parents, brother, and sister in our home in Alberta, old Canada. Dad runs the family lumber mill with Mom's oversight. The business has been in the family for four generations, and a dozen of my uncles, brothers, and cousins are on the payroll. My brother Richard runs a construction company that builds houses with Dad's lumber. My sister, Peggy, is a veterinarian. She's married with three children of her own."

Red shifted in his chair and continued, "Dad always wanted me to join him, but when I told him I wanted to go to the academy, he was very supportive. He even helped with getting recommendation letters for my nomination. I did very well on my competition exams. That, plus grades and football, were enough for a ticket to Mars. We had a great party before I left. I miss them like crazy," Red heaved a sigh. "What about your family?"

"I was lucky to get into the academy based mainly on my academic record and exam results. I didn't play sports in school. Instead, I had a job in data storage with UP Interplanetary Communications to help support my grandmother."

"That's tough."

"Who are all those girls?"

"Admirers," said Red with a grin.

"All from your hometown?"

"As far away as Earth and as near as Jupiter Station," he laughed. "It's something that defies explanation."

Gallant smiled at the redheaded giant and returned to concentrating on the chess match.

It didn't do much good. In three more moves, Red leaned back in his chair with a smirk. "Check."

"I yield," Gallant said, quickly calculating the inevitable mate, and surrendered his king.

"Not bad, but how about a little advice?" asked Red.

"I'd appreciate any pointers," said Gallant.

"You have good instincts and a keen mind. Your play was aggressive without being reckless. But your strategic viewpoint is weak."

"Strategic viewpoint? What do you mean?"

"Think of it this way; both white and black start the game with the same pieces, in the same position across a symmetric field. The only difference is that white moves first. It's that initial advantage that gives white an edge. Black must counter each white move to diminish that advantage while looking for an opportunity to create his advantage."

"Sure, OK," said Gallant. "So ...?

"Don't think of the opening moves as an immediate thrust to victory."

"Oh?"

"The opening moves are about creating a new configuration on the board, one where you create your own advantaged position. Your opening is merely a stepping stone to set up the dynamic that leads to mate. It's a matter of patience and timing."

"Thanks, Red. I'll keep that in mind for our next game," said Gallant.

"Great, that was fun. Now, I need something physical. So I'm heading to the gym. What about you? Want to come?"

"Sounds good to me," Gallant said enthusiastically.

It only took a few minutes to change their

clothes. Then, in the ship's gym, Red went straight to the weight machine while Gallant started jogging on one of the many treadmills.

As he worked up a sweat, Gallant looked around the large compartment.

To his chagrin, he noticed Kelsey and Neumann off to one side, jogging on neighboring treadmills, chatting amiably. Every time Kelsey's laugh erupted, Gallant felt a pang, but Kelsey never acknowledged he was there.

WHO'S THERE

9

Gallant developed his advanced fighter pilot skills while training for OOD qualification over the next few weeks.

He loved flying stunts in his Eagle but quickly learned that the neural headgear required intense concentration to fine-tune his thoughts. Pilots were trained to focus their mental energy and maintain that attention for extended periods. Under that kind of mental strain, pilots often burned out within a few years and had to be reassigned.

For Gallant, the demands of the neural headgear were particularly onerous. As a result, he often suffered migraine headaches after long sessions. But he managed to keep his pain to himself, so none of his shipmates noticed.

On one training flight, Gallant was deployed in a fighter screen covering *Repulse,* flying wingman for Red, the Flight 4 leader. Kelsey was in the seat behind his astrogator.

"Flight 4, take the anchor," the OOD ordered from the command center.

"Roger," responded Red. He switched channels. "Okay, Henry, guide on me."

Gallant tapped his microphone twice in response—*click ... click*.

The dozen Squadron 111 fighters had spread out in a lattice formation. Gallant and Red were on the sun-side flank of the fighter screen as the anchor node. The lattice extended a single ship's radar range by collecting signals from multiple nodes. This integrated the results into a collective image that included objects otherwise hidden within a planet's shadow.

Repulse reported, "We're picking up a new contact, designated as Alpha 23; located just behind the horizon of Europa. Flight 4, investigate. Flight 3, extend your flight trajectory to provide support as required."

"Aye aye, sir," replied Red and swung his Eagle out of the formation.

Gallant followed as Flight 3, Neumann and Chui, positioned themselves between Flight 4 and *Repulse*.

After confirming the location and flight path, Red reported to *Repulse*, "Alpha 23 appears to be a small Titan ship, destroyer class."

The Titan destroyer was about one-seventh the length of *Repulse*, but six times as long as an Eagle. The saucer had a sizeable domed center section.

Two years earlier, a UP survey ship had made first contact with an alien in orbit around Saturn's moon Titan. Unfortunately, the alien ship refused to communicate, so no one knew if the aliens were native to the solar system or visitors from another star. With no other point of reference, UP began referring to the aliens as Titans.

"Flight 4, close on the target. *Repulse* will maneuver to support you."

"Roger," acknowledged Red.

Once the aliens realized they had been discovered, they altered course and accelerated away from the Eagle.

Watching his screen for any reaction, Gallant armed his pulse lasers and Mongoose antimissiles.

The *Repulse* broadcast, "Unidentified ship, this is United Planet's, Jupiter Fleet. Identify yourself and state your purpose in this vicinity."

Instead of replying, the alien fired a plasma blast at Flight 4.

Gallant felt a surge of adrenaline and held his breath. Then, loosening his grip on the fighter's manual controls, he felt the ship's subtle response as he tightened his mental control. But the Titan's plasma blast dissipated before it reached the fighters.

This isn't at all like mock combat.

He said, "Red, I think that was just a warning shot."

Red responded, "Yeah, probably." He sharpened his course and increased his acceleration toward the target.

Gallant sensed Red's adjustments and guided his ship to maintain its wing position.

Could this encounter turn deadly?

They were closing the distance to the Titan craft, but *Repulse* interrupted them. "Do not pursue. Break contact and return to *Repulse*. Repeat, do not pursue."

Gallant bit back a curse and followed Red back to *Repulse*.

The Titan moved out of Jupiter's orbit and set a course toward the outer planets.

Gallant's neural headset was wet with sweat, and his head throbbed. He could hardly wait to complete the debriefing and get to his bunk. As he crumpled onto his bunk, he closed his eyes and again saw the plasma blast from the alien ship. Based on his academy training, he judged its maneuvers and actions to be sharp and professional. That was keeping with a scout ship prepared to defend itself but would not provoke hostilities.

Their refusal to communicate troubled him, but he was sure of one thing—they would be back.

MIND REVOLUTION

10

After an interminable day of division reports, followed by a humdrum evening as JOOD, Gallant returned to his cubicle to find Red changing into his gym gear.

"Hey, Red, wait up. I'll join you," said Gallant, stripping off his uniform and grabbing his gym outfit from his locker. "I need to work up a sweat."

"Sure, I know what you mean. I just finished six mind-numbing hours sitting on a lumpy chair in engineering. With all the AI power available, you would think an EOOW could do something more meaningful than watching the reactor parameters dance around with every power fluctuation. I am so ready to let off some steam."

They left the common room and began jogging

toward the gym. The jog quickly turned into a race, with just enough good-natured elbowing and genial shoving to keep it from getting severe.

They burst into the gym, out of breath and laughing, invigorated by the friendly competition.

"The only reason you won was that those scrawny legs let you hug the corners," laughed Red. He leaned against the bulkhead, huffing.

"I'm glad you found an excuse for your dismal performance," retorted Gallant, gasping for his share of air.

When they had recovered enough, they looked around the nearly empty gym. Red went straight for the punching bag. Gallant saw Kelsey jogging on the track that ran around the perimeter and sprinted toward her.

"Hi," said Gallant as he caught up and matched her pace. She glanced over, and a smile flickered across her lips. They jogged side by side without speaking for a while, content merely to share the space. The WHUMP! WHUMP! WHUMP! WHUMP! of Red's punching bag provided a rhythmic background for jogging, and the two kept up with the brisk pace Red maintained for nearly half an hour. Finally, he stepped away from the bag just as they passed him.

"How about a water break?" he panted.

Pulling three bottles of water from a dispenser, Gallant laughed at the sight. All three of them, with their breathing, labored, chests heaving, arms dragging, and shirts soaked with sweat. They sat on workout machines, gulping water and air with equal intensity.

"I think yoga might help your training program," suggested Kelsey, looking at Red.

"This body wasn't meant for those kinds of contortions."

"Your lopsided dimensions shouldn't be a serious impediment," she said with a grin, enjoying the chance to bait the oversized pilot.

"You're the one who's size-challenged." He stretched out a long arm to pat her on the head. "Anyway, why are you picking on me? Henry's the one who's a freak," he chuckled.

"Don't pull your punches, Red," she said, her grin expanding into a broad smile, "let Henry have it!"

"And why am I a freak?" asked Gallant. He looked from Red to Kelsey and back to Red.

"C'mon, Henry, don't be so sensitive," said Red, giving him a friendly poke. "You must know everyone talks about you behind your back. So, you should be open to discussing your peculiarities with your friends."

"What Red is trying to say," Kelsey said a little more tactfully, "is that you need to change how you think about yourself, Henry. You're not just a *little* different," she paused and pursed her lips, searching for the right words. "From our perspective, you're unique. You're one in a billion."

Gallant didn't reply.

"Henry, Henry, Henry, how can I explain?" she asked. "Every midshipman pilot on this ship can fly an Eagle. The neural interface lets them fly a huge, powerful antimatter space fighter, literally traveling at many kilometers per second with their thoughts."

"It took a century to develop that technology," replied Gallant, a defensive edge to his voice.

"Sure. It started with chips implanted in the brain," said Red.

Kelsey moved closer to Gallant. "Then genetic engineering, which had only been used to eliminate congenital disabilities and disease, was transformed. Designer enzymes and hormones radically altered brain chemistry. Today, those chemicals allow pilots to network with AI machines, through their neural interface."

"That's my point," said Red, getting excited. "After a century of trying, only those who were genetically enhanced could make the neural interface function." Then, after an awkward moment, he added, "Until you."

"That's why you're special. You were born to be a fighter pilot—a Natural," concluded Kelsey. "The question everyone wants to know is, are you a once-in-a-century affair or the first of a new kind? You have to admit; it's an intriguing question."

"That's why you got into the academy. That's why you're here. That's why Caine was so interested in you during the mock battle. You're always being watched," said Red, sucking his cheeks until he had squished his face into a prune.

"Now you're exaggerating," said Gallant, but he looked over his shoulder.

"Henry, you've got to think big. This is the

century of genetic mind enhancement. It happens, however, that some are more talented than others. That's why we're not all pilots," said Kelsey, suddenly self-conscious.

"Think of it as a sociological revolution," said Red, spreading his arms wide to illustrate the scope of the issue.

"You mean like the Industrial Revolution?" asked Gallant.

Kelsey touched Gallant's shoulder. "Exactly. Only our twenty-second-century mind revolution started with genetically enhanced neural interfaces. You may be the forerunner of something different. You herald a future where control of AI machines can be accomplished without genetic engineering. Control by pure thought. That's why Neumann resents you so much."

"Oh, you've noticed that?"

She nodded. "You're stealing his spotlight."

Gallant had fallen asleep when he heard Red yelp, snapping him back to wakefulness. "Hey, stop poking me! What do you want?"

"Mr. Gallant? Mr. Gallant?" a voice whispered.

"He's in the upper," growled Red, rolling over.

"Oh, I'm sorry, sir. Uh . . . Mr. Gallant?" said the intruder, redirecting his attention to the top bunk. "It's Chief Howard, sir. Wake up. I need you in the communications shack. We're getting an emergency data feed from a space probe. Do you hear me? Mr. Gallant . . . ?"

"Lights," said Gallant, and the room brightened as he sprang from his bunk. He shoved one leg into his trousers and one arm into his shirt, even as he reached for his shoes.

"Can I come too?" asked Red, throwing off his blanket.

Howard looked at Gallant with a shrug.

Gallant said, "Get dressed," but didn't wait for Red to catch up. Instead, he followed Howard out the door, and together, they dashed to CIC.

Still, Red arrived just a few seconds later.

Howard said, "Hagman, explain the nature of the data dump to Mr. Gallant."

"Yes, Chief," said Hagman. "Sir, we're receiving a directional burst transmission from Deep Space Probe 161. That probe has been on surveillance near Saturn for the past four months. Seven minutes ago, it began transmitting an unscheduled data dump. Dumps were only scheduled for the first of each month to optimize the trade-off between stealth and data collection. We only get unscheduled dumps if the AI system identifies an emergency. It would have to be either an uncontrollable equipment failure or if the probe has been detected. In either case, the probe transmits a complete data dump and then self-destructs."

Gallant tapped his comm pin and said, "Captain."

He had to wait only a few seconds for a groggy reply. "Captain here.".

"Captain, we have an unscheduled data dump from a probe conducting recon on Saturn."

"On my way."

Gallant stepped away from the compartment's entrance and tugged at Red's loose shirt. Unfortunately, he only succeeded in moving Red when Caine burst into the compartment.

"Go ahead with your report, Hagman," said Gallant.

"Yes, sir. The initial information was pretty standard, nothing out of the ordinary. But then we started getting some unusual images and statistics." Hagman wiped his brow nervously, not accustomed to being the center of attention of his commanding officer.

Chief Howard spoke up. "Captain, Midshipman Mitchel is on duty in CIC Analysis. She can compare the new data with our last evaluated situation report."

Caine nodded.

"I'll get her," said Gallant, stepping out and motioning Kelsey to come over.

Kelsey had been monitoring the flurry of activity from her CIC station and was ready. She bustled in and plugged a memory clip into the console. Charts and columns of numbers appeared in front of them.

"Captain, this is the most recent data analysis. You were briefed on most of it just two days ago," said Kelsey. She worked furiously to integrate her analyzed data against the additional information.

Caine ran one hand impatiently over his close-cropped hair while his other hand smoothed his rumpled uniform. The thought occurred to Gallant that Caine must have been sleeping in it.

"You can see here," Kelsey said, pointing to the virtual display, "we organized the information by satellites for each planet. So, Saturn, Neptune, Uranus, and Pluto estimates include the alien bases and ships."

"You mean guesses, don't you, Midshipman?" asked Caine with a resigned smile.

"Well, sir, I've often heard you say that an expert's educated guess can be nearly as good as a fact."

Caine blinked but didn't respond.

Kelsey tried to mask a disappointed look. "Should I call Lieutenant Mather, sir?"

"You can fill in your department head later, Midshipman Mitchel. But, right now, I want your expert opinion," said Caine.

Her confidence restored, Kelsey said, "The estimates I gave you two days ago were for the Titans' infrastructure. Some preliminary assumptions were included about their military strength. Here you can see the number of energy emission sites. They show communities, industries, and mining operations in many locations. Our population estimates range from one to ten million just for Saturn's satellites. We have a few rough estimates for Uranus but have been unsuccessful in getting a probe to Neptune or Pluto. I believe the Titans have extensive sensor arrays near those locations. Unfortunately, the probes self-destruct before we can collect any information."

"Yes, I see. Now show me the overlay of the new data."

She adjusted the virtual display. "Our previous population estimates don't suggest a long-term civilization on the outer planets. That is unless there are billions more aliens underground. But then they would need a huge underground industry, too. I guess they have inhabited Saturn's moons for less than a century. The Titans' planet of origin must be further out. These updated images don't add much to the statistics collected from our past information." She stopped to understand what she was seeing. "Hmm . . . the transmission terminated abruptly. We didn't receive the termination output. There doesn't appear to be much new here, Captain."

Caine said, "Things may not be what they appear."

"If the aliens would only communicate in some way . . ." said Kelsey.

Caine said, "The president has requested exchanging representatives. We've gotten no response from either official channels or our encounters with their scout ships."

Gallant thought they seemed to think the mere act of communicating would disadvantage them somehow.

Caine ordered, "We need accurate intelligence, or we'll get an unpleasant surprise. Mr. Gallant, prepare to launch another probe toward Saturn. Midshipman Mitchel, help him set the parameters."

"Yes, sir. I would also like to try another probe to

Neptune. If we strip it down to bare bones, we might be able to get it through whatever sensors they've deployed. That will mean a slow voyage, though," said Kelsey.

"All right, coordinate that with Mr. Gallant, too. I think it's time we came up with a few surprises of our own," Caine said with a cagey look.

An hour later, Gallant and Red returned to their quarters.

Red said, "You saw the images. Hundreds of ships around Saturn, and we can't even guess how many are near the outer planets."

"I don't know what I saw. Kelsey classified most of them as cargo ships or transports. Only a hundred or so were possible warships."

"A hundred or so? Do you hear yourself? You say that like it's a good thing."

"What's your opinion of Captain Caine?" asked Gallant abruptly.

"He's a great CO. Why?"

"I think that before long, we're going to be glad he's in command of the Jupiter frontier," said Gallant.

LEVERAGE

11

The unrestrained sky permitted an expansive view of the heavens as Eagle Flights 3 (Neumann and Chui), and 4 (Red and Gallant) escorted Repulse's shuttlecraft to the research laboratory on Ganymede. The shuttlecraft carried Commander Jackson, the science department head, and her staff.

Landing beacons guided the ships to the moon's surface. They avoided the numerous lava flows and islands of volcanic cones that protruded from the rough terrain. They came to a smooth stop on the soft gravel-tar landing strip. As the spacecraft touched down, the Ganymede director and his team approached.

The *Repulse* study team consisted of four scientists, four pilots, and four astrogators. They disembarked in their pressurized suits and strode under the light gravity, only fourteen percent of

Earth's. Only the landing hangars and a few relatively small buildings were visible above the ground. The accelerator's magnets and long linear tubes were housed underground because of the danger of meteorites.

The research facilities on Ganymede included one of UP's largest antiprotons accelerators. However, a small fraction of the particle stream was diverted to the laboratory for experimentation and research.

"Welcome, Commander," said the laboratory's director, Dr. Edward Lawrence. "We're glad to have you and your team visit."

Lawrence was a small, middle-aged man with a foxlike face. Next to him, Commander Jackson's large frame and brusque manner seemed more imposing than usual.

"Thank you, Dr. Lawrence. We're glad to be here and excited to learn more about your recent experiments. Captain Caine hopes some of them can be transformed into technology that might make a difference on the Jupiter frontier. I hope you don't mind that I asked a few pilots and astrogators to join our evaluation team. Their agile minds and hands-on experience may provide insight for practical applications."

"Quite possibly, quite possibly. We're happy to have you observe our progress. A few of our more inspired researchers have produced some provocative results. So come along, come along! We have a great deal to show you."

Dr. Lawrence led the *Repulse* team on a tour of

the extensive underground facility. Gallant, Red, and Kelsey discussed the elaborate structural supports for the underground corridors. Neumann and Chui were close behind, listening attentively. At the first workshop, Lawrence waved his arm at the four scientists clustered in the doorway.

"We have three ongoing investigations that have produced promising results," he said enthusiastically. "In this workshop, our team has run successful experiments to increase the stealth capabilities. Elizabeth?"

A young, attractive woman who couldn't have been much older than Gallant stepped forward. She led them toward an impressive apparatus.

"We've developed camouflage technology to cloak an entire building. By coating the target object with a metamaterial of nano-implants, we can force electromagnetic waves to bend. The nano-implants bend light around the object, like the water in a river diverting around a boulder. This renders the object effectively invisible."

"Would it be possible to cloak a ship?" asked Jackson.

"Yes," said Elizabeth, "though it would take several months to install the apparatus on your battlecruiser. It's also quite bulky, as you can see, meaning it would take up a lot of space on the ship."

"Would it be possible to cloak the entire aboveground hangar and buildings?" asked Gallant, not considering whether the question was appropriate for his rank.

All eyes turned toward Gallant.

Elizabeth said, "Why yes, given the proximity to the existing experimental building. We should be able to cloak our entire aboveground facility in just a few weeks." Then, turning to Commander Jackson, she asked, "Is that something Captain Caine might want?"

With a withering glance at Gallant, Jackson said, "Yes, that would improve the defensive position of this laboratory."

Dr. Lawrence stepped forward, nodding, and smiling. "Very well, I'll make arrangements. Any other questions or suggestions? No? Let's move on to the next workshop."

At the second workshop, Dr. Lawrence waved his arms as if to gather them all together. "This experiment is called MASS. It produces a space-time distortion that briefly creates an intense gravity-well. Released at a given location, the device will alter the course of any passing ship by changing the curvature of local space-time."

"Could you elaborate on that?" asked Jackson.

"Kind of speed bump to slow or divert passing ships and missiles?" Neumann said at the same time.

"Exactly!"

"Well then, could we lay a string of these devices, like mines, in an enemy's path?" asked Neumann.

"Setting them off in front of an attacking force would send their missiles haywire and disorganize their fleet. Is that possible, Dr. Lawrence?" asked Jackson.

"Not only is it possible, but I will get this team building MASS devices for you immediately."

Lawrence's comm pin buzzed, interrupting their discussion. He listened to a private message and then turned to address the group. "We have a slight delay before the last presentation. Feel free to wander about the facility and meet some laboratory team members. Please meet up again at Section E-12, 1700 hours."

Dr. Lawrence rubbed his hands together as the *Repulse* group reassembled at 1700 hours, smiling like a Cheshire cat. "I've saved the best for last. The group has developed a new kind of weapon called a FASER cannon. It combines nuclear fission with lasers. As you know, LASER stands for Light Amplification by Stimulated Emission of Radiation. FASER stands for Fission Amplification by Stimulated Emission of Radiation.

"A laser works by pulsing light through a crystal so that the crystal releases a flood of identical electromagnetic waves all at once. Our experiment pulses light through a block of crystalline Uranium-235. That creates coherent photofission where all the Uranium-235 atoms fission simultaneously. It produces an energy beam of highly focused power.

"We have prepared a demonstration for your benefit," Dr. Lawrence said. "If you watch this display, we have targeted our FASER gun on a small asteroid."

He turned to the workshop team leader. "Are you ready?"

The man nodded, looking slightly nervous.

"Fire."

The team watched intently on the display as an energy beam fired into the asteroid, which instantly disintegrated into dust.

The *Repulse* team was very impressed. Unfortunately, the prototype was enormous, and Lawrence was reluctant to speculate on how long it would take to reduce the size. Nevertheless, they all agreed it could make an excellent weapon for protecting Ganymede.

Gallant wondered whether the weapon would be enough to protect Jupiter Station but kept his doubts to himself.

After the tour, Dr. Lawrence invited Jackson and her team to stay for dinner, an invitation they eagerly accepted. The research station had a reputation for treating special guests to delicacies typically unheard of so far out in the Solar System.

They weren't disappointed. The dining compartment was nondescript, but a long table full of food awaited the group, wafting tantalizing aromas.

The dinner started with a salad of real lettuce, tomatoes, cucumbers, olives, and dressing. It was a treat the *Repulse* members relished.

Dr. Lawrence explained, "Since we're so far from the sun, we use the moon's geothermal energy for power instead of solar arrays. We grow food in our hydroponic garden."

But most of the "oohs" and "ahs" came with the main course—broiled salmon, asparagus, potatoes, carrots, and several bottles of wine.

"We have a fish farm as well," said Dr. Lawrence, beaming with pride. "We're very fortunate here on Ganymede. It has a thin oxygen atmosphere and an iron-rich liquid core. Best of all, an actual saltwater ocean exists 250 kilometers below the surface, sandwiched between layers of ice and rock."

He looked at his attentive audience. "We discovered colonies of assorted creatures—giant tube worms, crustaceans, and others even stranger—clustered around undersea volcanic features known as black smokers. These creatures thrive without sunlight, existing as part of a food chain based on a bacterium that uses chemosynthesis. They are our extraterrestrial inhabitants. Of course, we don't eat these creatures; we study them. But we've extracted the water, purified it, and created farms for imported Earth fish."

Having survived mostly synthetic meals for so long, the *Repulse* team lavished praise on their hosts throughout the meal.

Gallant was enjoying a feast of fresh food which quickly soured when Neumann had claimed the seat on Kelsey's right.

Neumann said, "Someday, Kelsey, you must let

me take you sailing on the ocean. It's one of the pleasures unique to Earth."

"It sounds wonderful," she said. "Sailing, I mean."

"It's a family tradition. I practically grew up on my family's yacht. My dad feels that sailing develops a sense of adventure."

Gallant concentrated on his salmon until he saw Neumann take a big bite of carrots, providing an opening in the conversation. He asked, "Kelsey, you were raised on a farm. What do you think about hydroponics and fish farms in space?"

Kelsey's face lit up as she turned to him and dove into a detailed discourse on the life-affirming aspects of growing living things. Gallant asked questions and offered opinions to keep her attention focused on him. Before long, she raised her wine glass with a warm smile.

As she related a story, an expansive laugh escaped her lips, and she covered her mouth with her hands, eyes sparkling. The story was engaging, but her unrestrained joy in telling it made it especially appealing.

What's she thinking?

SEEK AND YOU
SHALL FIND

12

The colossal warship clawed her way around Jupiter, surveying the large retinue of moons. Blustering storms swirled on the gas giant's surface, forming a mosaic of vague images—any of which could have hung majestically in an art gallery. Raucous winds swept along the surface, singing their songs.

As *Repulse* traveled through Jupiter's thin rings, micrometeorites disintegrated against her hull. In the distance, small craft and merchantmen dotted the horizon. Three flights of Eagle fighters were soaring nearby in a lattice formation.

Gallant stood on the bridge of the *Repulse*, nearing the end of his JOOD watch. Usually, he savored the grandeur of the writhing planetary oceans, but today he was distracted by Kelsey's silhouette between him and the viewport.

Refocusing his attention on the current series of radar sweeps, he ordered, "Flights one, two, and three, reform into formation bravo." Then he added to the helmsman, "Hard to port, come to course 180, azimuth up 10 degrees, acceleration 0.001c, at time 11:55." He felt the ship respond, even while the fighters repositioned around her.

"Kelsey," he yelled over the din on the bridge. A wave of his hand beckoned her aft.

Balancing herself gracefully against the motion of the deck, she made her way to him. After her pre-watch walkthrough and review of the status board, she was prepared to relieve him as JOOD. Instead, he said to her, "We are conducting mobile radar sweeps around Jupiter. Our acceleration is 0.001 c, two hundred thousand kilometers from the planet. Two merchantmen and several shuttles are listed on the contact board—no maintenance or repair operations are in progress. I have the conn. The captain has the deck."

"No long-range sweeps?" she asked.

"That evolution will be on your watch section." He smiled, knowing she would be pleased to perform the complex scans facing the outer planets.

"Good," she said. "I relieve you." Her face was alight with anticipation for the upcoming maneuvers.

"I stand relieved," he said.

Raising her voice so the entire bridge could hear, she said, "This is Midshipman Mitchel. I am the

Junior Officer of the Deck. I have the conn."

"Very well," said Caine.

"Request permission to remain on the bridge to observe, sir?" asked Gallant, hoping to gain some experience on the long-range radar sweep.

"Permission granted, but stay out of the way," said Captain Caine.

"Yes, sir. Thank you, sir." Gallant moved to the starboard wing, relishing a few additional minutes on the bridge. As the bridge crew readied for the next maneuver, he let his mind wander.

Captain Caine ordered, "Midshipman Mitchel, prepare for long-range sweeps."

"Aye aye, sir," said Kelsey.

Kelsey reviewed the virtual screen that displayed the lattice configuration. Then, she coordinated her calculations with the AI on how to reposition *Repulse.*

Gallant followed her math, well accustomed to doing the calculations in his head.

The goal of the long-range sweep was to scan for activity around the outer planets. Captain Caine had positioned his battlecruisers and fighters to ensure overlapping radar coverage.

Captain Caine watched, only checking to see that the crew kept on schedule. Then, satisfied that they were, he said, "Midshipman Mitchel, commence scan at time 1230 hours."

"Aye aye, sir," she replied.

Kelsey ordered, "All fighters, form lattice formation gamma-seven." She turned to the helmsman. "Come right to bearing 122 degrees, azimuth up 010 degrees, velocity 0.001 c, course 120, time 1230 hours."

Kelsey's astrogation was flawless. *Repulse* settled into the exact center of the lattice formation.

The exercise proceeded successfully, although the sweep revealed nothing new. Some bulk information was added to the disposition of ships around Saturn, but the details were poor, given the distance.

Chief Howard's voice boomed over the ship's intercom a few minutes later. "Captain, I've received the long-range radar results from the rest of the fleet and am forwarding the data to the bridge."

"Very well," responded the captain, striding to the radar station to see the results for himself. Each of the five battlecruisers sent data from their scans. It was up to *Repulse* to integrate all the information into a comprehensive picture of planetary space.

Gallant craned his neck to catch a peek, thinking about one of Caine's favorite sayings: "Proper planning prevents poor performance."

Captain Caine planned to optimize radar by using strategically placed arrays. He spread his ships' antennas across as vast an area as possible. The dispersed ships scanned Saturn to produce a superimposed result.

Although this system offered assurance that Jupiter could not be approached from the direction of the outer planets without detection, Neptune and

Uranus were on the other side of the sun and entirely outside the radar search area.

Division leaders Lieutenant Stahl and Lieutenant Mather reviewed the results. Then, as the findings were reported, *Repulse*'s CIC analyzed them.

Lieutenant Stahl said, "No indication of any large formations approaching from Saturn. The Titans seem to be content to stay in their backyard."

"Perhaps," said Caine.

Lieutenant Mather said, "We still have too many Titan destroyers patrolling the asteroid belt. They might interfere with mining operations or interdict shipping."

"They haven't done so yet," said Caine. Nevertheless, after deliberating with Stahl and Mather, Caine considered the possibility more seriously.

Captain Caine turned to his communications officer, who snapped to attention. "Midshipman Gallant, draft the order for *Devastator* and *Dauntless*, immediate transmission. They're to move into the shallows of the asteroid belt. From that position, they are to evaluate all alien ships seen near the mining settlements."

"Aye aye, sir," said Gallant. His mind raced on how to word the orders. He wondered what impact moving two battlecruisers would have on the fleet.

CONTACT

13

Several weeks later, Gallant reported to the captain's cabin. "Junior Officer of the Deck, sir. The Officer of the Deck sends his respects and reports a distant radar contact approaching Jupiter at high velocity."

Captain Caine had just sat down to his breakfast —a cup of strong, steaming, real coffee, two real eggs over-easy, crisp bacon, and toast with strawberry jam—made especially for his birthday. The delicious aroma made Gallant's stomach rumble.

The captain frowned at the interruption. Gallant wasn't sure whether he was more disturbed about the possibility of an enemy invasion or forfeiting his birthday meal. He took a large bite of eggs and chewed them deliberately before speaking.

"Thank you," Caine said as he pushed away from the table. He briefly checked his local computer readout before following Gallant.

Caine was still buttoning his jacket as he opened the stateroom hatch. He had barely secured the last button as he acknowledged the salute of the Marine guard stationed outside.

Taking two stairs at a time, he bounded up the ladder.

"Report," said Caine as he strode onto the bridge.

"Captain, we have a contact at four hundred million kilometers, on a flight trajectory toward Jupiter. It must be a huge formation, hundreds of alien ships, to register this significantly. ETA is ten days," responded the OOD.

Caine considered the distance to the aliens. They could be coming from any of the sixty-two moons of Saturn. They could have started from Uranus or Neptune.

Caine said, "Mr. Gallant, signal Mars Fleet Command and inform them of a possible major attack on Jupiter Station in ten days."

From his position at the communications station, Gallant transmitted the message. The eighty-six-minute delay seemed interminable.

The Mars Fleet Command responded, "Mars Fleet is being placed on alert but will remain to defend Mars. Collect all available ships in your area to defend Jupiter at all costs."

The captain nodded. "That's what I expected. Even if they could send help, at flank acceleration Mars Fleet reinforcements would take sixteen days to reach Jupiter."

He drummed his fingers on the arm of his chair for a moment, then said, "Send a general recall to all ships between Mars and Jupiter. Tell them to rendezvous with *Repulse*."

Caine looked over at Gallant and asked, "What's your best estimate on which ships can respond in time?"

Gallant tapped at his computer panel to identify the last known positions of the ships and said, "*Renown* and *Remarkable*." Then, he hesitated before adding, "Possibly *Retribution*, along with six or seven destroyers."

"That's all?"

"Yes, sir."

Caine nodded, considering the fleet's battle characteristics and assessing its strength.

Gallant wondered what four battlecruisers and a handful of destroyers could do to defend the outpost against such a massive attack force.

Renown, *Retribution*, and *Remarkable* were battlecruisers, the same class as *Repulse*. Their armament included eight bow, four aft missile tubes, ten short-range plasma weapons, and forty laser guns amidships. They were protected by armor belts, force shields, and electronic warfare decoys and sensors.

The missiles were both 'fire and forget' and remote guidance. The missiles included their sensors and decoys with a maximum acceleration of 0.1 c.

In addition to the artillery, each battlecruiser carried a dozen Eagle fighters.

The UP destroyers were a smaller version of

the battlecruisers. Each included four bow missile launchers and two mid-ship launchers. The missiles launched by a destroyer were only one-fourth of the explosive power of a battlecruiser's missile. In addition, the destroyers had six lasers but no plasma weapons or fighters.

Previous confrontations with the Titans had involved only one or two alien ships, usually with brief exchanges of missiles or laser fire. Some UP vessels were damaged, but Jupiter Fleet had learned little about the Titans' capabilities. The coming encounter would be the first real test against them.

Gallant looked up as Caine surveyed the bridge. *Repulse* was a mighty ship worthy of the captain's pride in his command. She had already won her spurs through many previous skirmishes with the aliens. The captain looked calm and resolute, confident in his ship and her mission, but Gallant was troubled that they faced too many unknowns.

MERCHANTS

14

As Gallant decoded the communications traffic over the next few hours, frantic calls for protection rang out. The twenty billion citizens of the United Planets relied on interplanetary trade. Each planet and colony contributed its unique assets to the civilization.

Several thousand cargo ships routinely transited between Earth and its neighboring planets. Another thousand ships moved within the asteroid belt. In addition, dozens of trade ships shuttled cargo around Jupiter's moons.

Until now, the alien ships had merely observed all this activity, but now the appearance of a large fleet stoked fears of an innovative approach. Gallant carried the latest action message by hand to Captain Caine.

"Action message, Captain."

Captain Caine sat with Commander Eddington,

reviewing the ship's general quarters bill. Both men froze momentarily, then Caine swung around in his chair to face Gallant and said, "Read it aloud."

"'Following Jupiter Fleet's general instructions and emergency procedures, NNR Inc. demands immediate escort for their merchant ship convoys.'"

He paused. "It's signed by both G. Neumann, President of NNR Inc., and Senator W. Graham."

Gallant recognized both names. Gerald Neumann was not merely Midshipman Anton Neumann's father but the owner of the largest company in the United Planets. Senator Graham was the leader of the Senate in the Interplanetary Congress.

"They didn't waste any time," said the XO, taking out a handkerchief and wiping his brow. He leaned back in his chair, the cushion groaning in protest.

"Gallant, show me the text of Fleet General Instructions and Emergency Procedures," said Caine.

Gallant tapped an icon on his tablet to display the text on the main viewer screen over the captain's desk. The captain and XO skimmed through it quickly.

"The provisions relevant to requests for emergency convoy escort are fairly clear," said the XO.

"Nevertheless, we have broad discretion regarding when, where, and how many escorts we provide. And I'm even the one who determines what constitutes hazardous circumstance," responded Caine.

"Captain, you can't ignore this. The demand

comes from Gerald Neumann himself. Senator Graham's co-signature merely emphasizes that he expects immediate compliance," said the XO.

"Let me see the classified orders we just received from Mars Fleet Headquarters."

Gallant was ready for the request. The orders appeared in seconds.

"Hmm . . . 'You are to defend Jupiter Station and the Ganymede support base at all costs.' 'AT ALL COSTS,' it says. That means with every ship and resource at my disposal." Caine let the point sink in, his eyes boring into Eddington's.

"NNR would argue that you should defend the station with every ship at your disposal *after* you dispatch an escort for their merchantmen," Eddington pointed out.

"They might say that, but any UP officer worth his uniform would keep the force united in the face of the enemy."

"Captain, I suggest we convene a videoconference with Rook, Minford, and Waller to make them aware of the situation," said the XO. "*Renown*, *Remarkable*, and *Retribution* need to know about the situation."

Caine said, "Which situation do you mean—the alien fleet or the merchantmen convoy request?"

The XO shrugged. "Both. If you outline our objectives and your action plan, perhaps they'll have helpful suggestions."

Caine grunted, indicating he already knew how helpful their suggestions would be. He said, "Mr.

Gallant, set up a videoconference with the captains of the other battlecruisers. I want it running in this room in thirty minutes. Chief Howard can monitor from the communications shack, but I want you here during the conference in case of any signal interruptions."

"Aye aye, sir," said Gallant, hustling back to the communications shack to make the arrangements. He was thrilled at the opportunity to be privy to the latest intelligence and the private thoughts of senior fleet officers.

Thirty minutes later, he returned. "The videoconference is ready, Captain." He tapped the captain's screen to display images of the three captains, adding, "There is a slight time delay between ships, sir."

Caine began, "Gentlemen, I recalled you to Jupiter Station because we identified a large fleet heading toward Jupiter. Our orders are to defend Jupiter Station and the colonies at all costs. In addition, we now have a request to provide NNR convoy escorts. I plan to defend Jupiter Station using all four battlecruisers and seven destroyers. They have forty-eight combined fighters. I intend to deploy the fighters in a primarily defensive role to destroy incoming missiles. I will wait for the aliens to make the first move and attack them only if they threaten the colonies. I'm ordering the Marines to defend Jupiter Station, the Ganymede Research Lab, and the Ganymede capital, Kendra."

Gallant sat monitoring the communications

setup while listening to the conversation.

Rook said, "Finally, an opportunity to engage the aliens in a serious contest! Maybe they won't just fire a few shots and run away this time. But why wait for them at Jupiter Station? Once our ships assemble, we should attack. We will show them our strength and send them back to the outer planets where they belong with a clear lesson they won't forget."

Minford said, "We must consider the political consequence of our disposition. We need to evacuate essential members of the civilian population with the NNR convoy. That will reassure the remaining colonists and guarantee the mine owners that they will not be left to the vagaries of the enemy. Of course, providing substantial escorts for the convoy is undeniably important. Those people are the lifeblood of our supply chain. The president of NNR and Senator Graham would not look kindly on . . . well, anything happening to them. Besides, what if the aliens are only making a feint toward Jupiter Station? They could skim right past our fleet toward Mars with their acceleration advantage. That would leave us kilometers behind while they blast every merchant ship along the way."

Wow! The captains have different perspectives.

Caine said, "We will engage the battle at the time and place of our choosing, not theirs. And that place is here, by Jupiter Station. We have our orders to protect the citizens and facilities in orbit. Mars Fleet can take care of itself. We will not make special arrangements for political leaders to flee the area. Nor will we divert a substantial portion of our force to escort merchantmen. Not when hundreds of thousands of women and children would be left to the mercy of the Titans. The colonists will evacuate and go to underground shelters, trusting the Marines for protection. I hope to use Jupiter Station's missile battery and the research lab's FASER cannon for defense. Those should surprise our opponents. We will defend the area and drive off any threats with a united force."

Waller said, "We must prevent any threat to the Ganymede population and defeat the Titans. I believe Captain Caine's plan is the best one to accomplish this."

So do I.

Rook said, "We don't know how powerful the enemy force is. We have very little information about them at all. We have no idea what systems they have, whether they use AI, or how such systems would operate in battle. How they think is as important as how many ships they have."

Caine said, "If we can gather intelligence on their capabilities we will, but we must consider those secondary issues. Defense is our primary concern."

Just before the videoconference ended, Minford said, "Together, we can meet all our obligations. But we must be united."

A half-hour later, in the communications

shack, Gallant heard Eddington's voice from around the corner. "Where are *Dauntless* and *Devastator*?" Standing just inside the communications shack door, Gallant pricked up his ears.

"They're deep inside the asteroid belt, too far to reach us before the Titans arrive. So, we'll have to face them with four battlecruisers instead of six," Mather replied.

The XO thumped his fist against the desk. "I warned him not to split the fleet. His plan to cast the widest possible search net was risky right from the start. We'll pay for that decision."

Mather grunted, "What do you think he'll do about Neumann's demand for escorts?"

"You know his history. He came up from the ranks and worked himself silly. That's how he wound up the senior captain on the station. It took him forever to get this command. His wife, children, and grandchildren all live on Mars. Most of them work for the NNR shipping company in one capacity or another. He once defied Gerald Neumann over shipyard procurement, costing him his promotion to admiral. Senator Graham might look to have him relieved if he doesn't comply with Neumann's demands this time."

Mather sighed, "He's always been a risk-taker. Usually, his risks pay off."

The XO said, "True, but not always. Risk is one thing; rashness is something else. Case in point, we're going into action light two battlecruisers."

PROBE

15

wo days later, *Renown* and *Remarkable* joined *Repulse* in orbit around Ganymede near Jupiter Station.

The battlecruisers carried powerful multiwarhead anti-ship missiles called Hydra-IIIs. Each Hydra-III was armed with six W762 warheads. There were designed for use against capital spaceships with yields of seventeen megatons per warhead. The missiles used a combination of inertial guidance and radar homing. They had multi-radiation detection homing devices and external laser painting. Autonomous onboard targeting systems independently acquired targets using embedded artificial intelligence.

The ships had to refuel after their extended journey. So, before entering orbit, they docked at Jupiter Station to restock their supply of antimatter.

Gallant stood in the doorway to the

midshipmen's common room and spoke loudly to be heard over the din. "Refueling could be the reason for the threat of attack."

The refueling activity had been a constant topic of conversation. The room was crowded with midshipmen, most of them off-duty and dressed casually, though a few coming up on watch duties were in uniform. The clamor of numerous conversations filled the room.

Neumann was seated at the large table across from Gallant in full uniform. He folded his arms and scowled. The other midshipmen stared at Gallant, stunned at his nerve. Except for Red and Kelsey, few of them had spoken to Gallant outside of professional requirements since his first day onboard. Gallant had performed well enough to avoid direct censure from his shipmates, but Neumann never tired of challenging him.

For the most part, Gallant had learned to avoid confrontation and ignore those who ignored him. But now he stood firm, eyes darting around the room, daring his shipmates to discount his opinion.

"What do you mean by that?" asked Barrington, unable to contain her curiosity.

Neumann practically quivered in his seat as if to protest the violation of Gallant's informal verbal isolation.

"That Titan scout we chased off several weeks ago might have discovered the new accelerator on Ganymede. They realize it will allow us to produce our antimatter, which extends our refueling capabilities at the station. We now can conduct extended multiple ship journeys toward Saturn and Neptune. They would see that as a threat," said Gallant.

"That's only possible if you think the aliens have considerable knowledge of our ships," countered Neumann.

"I think the aliens may have been in this system for quite some time, monitoring human progress for decades. We know they have a sizeable population and numerous ships on Saturn's satellites," said Gallant.

"If that's true, and they were hostile, why didn't they attack long ago?" persisted Neumann.

"Maybe they're originally from another star. In that case, they would have had to build shipyards and support facilities before attacking."

"Why couldn't they use the interstellar ships you imagine they have?" Neumann spoke heatedly. He stood up and leaned forward, almost in Gallant's face.

Gallant said, "If the Titans started on a generation ship from one of our neighboring stars, their intent could have been to seed a colony. But, instead, once they got to our solar system, they discovered it was already inhabited."

"Why didn't they try to communicate with us?" asked Chui.

"All of their interactions with us have been hostile. So maybe they're just an aggressive and dangerous species," said Neumann.

Kelsey asked, "Does anyone have an idea what kind of fleet tactics they'll employ?"

"The aliens have been content to fire a few

warning shots and leave," said Red, "but we've never seen any fighters. Their ships have all been destroyer or cruiser size."

"Tell me, Gallant, do you think our fighters could defeat their destroyers, one on one?" asked Neumann.

"Even though they're small, a Titan destroyer would outmatch a single fighter. The destroyer would likely have ship-killer missiles and heavy plasma weapons. Our lasers and antimissile missiles don't pack enough punch to inflict more than moderate damage," responded Gallant.

Many questions remained unanswered.

Some answers came sooner than expected.

That evening Deep Space Probe 162 began transmitting data to *Repulse*. Finally, after its four-week journey, the replacement probe reached Saturn and gathered information.

CIC teemed with scientists, analysts, and technicians. They tried to make sense of the uploaded data and spout opinions on the best course of action.

Commander Jackson said, "Based on the analysis, Titan was chosen because of the moon's favorable environment."

Kelsey said, "While Saturn has a hydrogen-helium atmosphere, Titan has its atmosphere. It is primarily nitrogen with less than two percent methane and hydrogen. It's bigger than Mercury and covered with hydrocarbon clouds. A methane cycle was a complex molecular soup. It was formed when ultraviolet radiation reacted with the methane in its upper atmosphere. The probe's data indicate that the surface has black, oily rivers and lakes of methane at one hundred eighty degrees Kelvin."

Jackson said, "Worlds like Titan, with temperatures suitable for liquid methane, are often found around a red dwarf star. One possibility for the aliens' home planet could be Gliese 581, an M3-type red dwarf located 20.5 light-years away. We've confirmed four planets orbiting Gliese 581. Life in this environment would be a whole new category, where liquid methane replaces our liquid water cycle. Such lifeforms would take in H_2 rather than O_2 and produce methane instead of carbon dioxide."

Gallant speculated, "Perhaps the outer gas giants are what attracted them to our system. This data suggests that the Titans are terraforming or, in this case, 'Gliese-forming' our outer planets. They may have little desire to approach Earth or any inner planets. But as interlopers, they'd likely assume they would have to fight us for them. So, they don't want to communicate and give away any information."

Since their last data dump, Kelsey estimated that many transports and warships had left Saturn's orbit. "The Titan force approaching Jupiter came from Saturn, which means their numbers there are depleted. More could still be coming from the outer planets. But my estimate—or guess, as the captain frames it—is that at least two hundred ships have left

Saturn."

"How many would you say are warships? And what are the rest, supply ships?" asked Gallant.

"About eighty percent are warships, and the rest could be a combination of transports and supply ships," Kelsey replied.

"Transports? Then this could well be an invasion force," he said.

"Most likely. Possibly twenty to thirty transports."

"They have a space station at Titan with a field generator that distorts their emissions, and it's tough to evaluate. The aliens aim to misdirect and surprise us with their actual strength as much as possible," said Gallant.

"Look at these images around Titan. Would you say those objects are orbital fortresses?" asked Kelsey.

Howard said, "The probe has been collecting emissions from the ships to identify them, but it's also collecting communications. So, we can't make any sense out of those signals."

"That can't be right. You mean you can't decrypt or decode them?" asked Gallant.

"The signals combine dots, dashes, musical tones, frequency oscillations, and harmonics in patterns we don't grasp. I mean, I can't tell whether it's a language, an encrypted language, or their music videos," said Howard.

"At least we have some time to prepare," said Kelsey.

"Regardless, it's safe to say this will be a massive

attack that will test our strength," said Gallant.

Captain Caine arrived in time to hear Gallant's statement.

He said, "Mr. Gallant, I want you and Midshipman Mitchel to go to Ganymede and brief Colonel Ridgewood of the Seventh Marines. Send Chief Howard to set up a communications satellite, so Ridgewood can stay in contact with *Repulse* while he's in the underground bunkers."

***

Landing beacons guided Flight 4 and a shuttlecraft to the touchdown pad for the Ganymede Research Laboratory. As soon as they landed, Chief Howard and his communications team went straight to work, setting up the relay link.

On their way to meet Colonel Ridgewood, Kelsey and Gallant passed civilian workers carrying out their daily tasks.

Kelsey commented, "You'd never guess they were facing an alien invasion."

Gallant said, "Pioneers are hardy stock. It takes a lot to shake them. So, I think they'll hold up well."

Dr. Lawrence and Colonel Ridgewood were waiting in the main conference room. The briefing was quick, and both men quickly grasped the essentials of the situation.

Ridgewood asked, "If there is an invasion, how much fleet support can I count on?"

"Captain Caine will make every effort to defend Ganymede, but it's likely the fleet will have its hands full," said Gallant. "The satellite relay to my team is being set up. It will let you stay in touch with the fleet during the action."

"What tactics will be most effective against these methane breathers?"

Kelsey said, "Their landing forces will undoubtedly wear body armor and their breathing apparatus. We believe they will fight with conventional hand laser and plasma weapons."

Ridgewood asked, "You don't think their fleet will conduct a nuclear bombardment?"

"Our analysis team doesn't believe so," said Kelsey.

"Why not?" asked Ridgewood, incredulous.

"For the same reason, they haven't already tried to bombard our colonies with nuclear weapons. Either they fear retaliation or have an ethical threshold, and genocide crosses the line for them, as it does for us. Commander Jackson feels this colony of Titans must still have elders back on their home planet. They would hold the Titans accountable for their behavior. That said, there is no assurance that the war couldn't escalate at some point," said Kelsey.

"Well, my marines will be ready for anything, including close-in combat. Our heavy-weapons company is deployed around the accelerator since it's critical to the fleet's long-term operations. Hopefully, the cloaking shield will hide the research facility and prevent a direct assault. Regardless, I'm deploying one battalion to defend the lab itself. Another battalion will defend Jupiter Station. The remaining unit will hold Ganymede's capital city, Kendra," said

Ridgewood.

"The civilian population throughout the Jupiter colonies is preparing. They are stocking food and life-support supplies. Then, we will transport them to their underground shelters," said Dr. Lawrence.

After the briefing, Gallant and Kelsey went to find Chief Howard. But unfortunately, the communications team wasn't quite finished with the array, so the two midshipmen went to see Jake's son, Sergeant Bernstein.

They found him on the gun range, checking his weapon sights using an AI-controlled rifle to identify and center on targets. They watched as he fired pellet rounds, laser beams, and plasma blasts from different available magazines. After introductions and pleasantries, he asked, "So, you know my dad?"

"I met him when I reported for duty," said Gallant. "I told him I'd look you up if I ever had a chance. He was very kind to me."

"That's Dad," the Marine said with pride.

The three of them chatted amiably for some minutes until Gallant's comm pin buzzed, Howard's signal that the team was almost ready to leave.

"Is there anything we can do for you?" Gallant asked the young sergeant.

"There is. My family is scattered across the colonies out here. With restricted communications these days, it's impossible to contact individuals. Would it be too much to ask for you to try to get a message to my wife and kids on Europa?" asked Bernstein.

"Don't worry; I can find them. You can record your message on this memory stick," said Gallant confidently.

Bernstein stepped aside and quietly recorded his message. His face was sad as he pressed the recording into Gallant's hand.

"Thank you."

On returning to the shuttle, Kelsey and Gallant stopped by the laboratory's huge viewing dome to find Red. With Red's arm protectively around her shoulder, he and Elizabeth sat close together.

OVERTURE

16

Captain Caine prepared his fleet to face the enemy. He ordered all ships to conduct system checks, repair essential equipment, and update maintenance. They were to complete any last-minute training of personnel.

Gallant was standing JOOD watch on the bridge when Caine looked him up and down and said, "Mr. Gallant, I'm going to need every starfighter I have over the next week. However, I also need an escort for the civilian evacuation convoy. So, your squadron will escort the convoy partway to Mars."

Surprised that the captain had chosen to reveal his thoughts to him, Gallant asked, "What about the Titan fleet, sir?"

"That's a calculated risk. You must see the convoy out of harm's way and return to Repulse before the aliens reach the station."

"When do we leave, sir?"

"As soon as the merchant convoy is fully formed —about twenty-four hours."

Caine took a deep breath and added, "Make the most of your free time until then. It's likely to be the last you'll get until . . ."

The setting sun cast a glow through the dome window as Gallant pulled open the ornate glass door of the Lobster Tavern. It was an upscale restaurant in Jupiter Station's entertainment district. Beside him, Red entered the cocktail lounge, extravagant for any building so far from Earth. Staff bustled around the room, ensuring the last-minute touches were completed for the evening's activities.

The main room had been reserved for Squadron 111's party as the last liberty before their convoy escort mission. The young officers arrived a few times in civilian attire, with their previous month's pay burning a hole in their pockets. Prices for farm-grown lobster and drinks promised to deplete those funds soon enough.

Kelsey Mitchel wore casual slacks and a UPSA sweatshirt. She sat in the center of the room, tapping her fingers impatiently on the tabletop. Her hazelnut hair was pulled back in a ponytail that cascaded across her left shoulder, but her face wore a look of impatient annoyance. Her classic features made her the most striking woman in the room.

Unceasingly, men she knew and locals she

didn't came over and tried to join her.

"Hi," she said repeatedly. "It's great to see you, but I'm waiting for someone." Then she would tilt her head to one side and flash a luminescent smile that suggested she was disappointed and hoped he would understand. This placated most, but one hopeful suitor kept hovering. When she finally spotted Gallant and Red, she stood up, waving excitedly. As they approached, the persistent admirer withdrew with a glare at them.

Red took the chair on Kelsey's right and Gallant on her left. Something about this arrangement felt vaguely familiar and unsettling to Gallant. His tousled hair, casual shirt and khakis, and fresh-faced naiveté attracted a waitress's attention. She came by to take their order.

"Beer all around," said Red, eager to get started on the celebration.

As soon as their drinks arrived, Red raised his mug and said, "Here's to us."

The three clicked mugs, downed the beer, and thudded the empty glasses on the table in unison.

"Again!" shouted Red, to the waitress.

She laughed, waved her hand in acknowledgment, and went to fill the order. The crowd was growing. The combination of civilian garb and alcohol had its predictable effects. The mood in the room was gay and boisterous.

Sandy Barrington entered the restaurant and crossed the room with quick, deliberate steps. She stopped at Gallant's table to say hello, but her eyes scanned the room and locked on the far corner.

Gallant looked past the overexcited crowd to see what had distracted her. Neumann and Chui were sitting at the table, looking grim and sad.

Grim and Somber — that could be their names.

Neumann's good looks and fashionable civilian attire attracted stares from many of the young ladies in the room.

Sandy gazed at Neumann. They exchanged a wink, a gesture, an unspoken word, then she turned and glared at Kelsey.

Gallant had a sudden flash of insight into their triangular relationship.

Sandy moved toward the contentious corner and sat next to Neumann. They began what looked to be a heated conversation.

After a few moments, Gallant's attention returned to his table, and their waitress arrived with another round of beer. He had no sooner filled his mouth with brew than Ed Stevenson came up from behind and slapped him on the back.

Gallant struggled to get the beer down without spewing it over his friends, then stood up to greet his friend.

"Thanks," he coughed, giving Ed a hearty handshake.

He said, "Red, Kelsey, this is Ed Stevenson, one of my roommates at the academy. He's stationed on *Renown*."

"Hi," Red and Kelsey said simultaneously.

"Kelsey, you must be Henry's astrogator. I've

heard so very little about you," Stevenson said with a roguish smile.

Gallant diverted the conversation by asking about the *Renown*. Stevenson plopped down, took a long swallow of Gallant's beer, and said, "I can't stay. I'm meeting some of my *Renown* shipmates. See you later." He downed the last of Gallant's drink and stood up with a smirk. "Hey, thanks for the beer."

"I'm sorry to see you leave, Ed," said Red. "I hoped to wheedle a few tales of Gallant's academy days from you before you left."

Kelsey laughed.

"Next time," said Stevenson. He waved and disappeared into the milling crowd.

Before long, some of the officers began to call Chui's name. At first, he waved them off, looking embarrassed, but he gave in and sat down at the bar's virtual piano. He started with popular tunes but soon shifted to oldies from a bygone era.

"Kel–sey! Kel–sey! Kel–sey!" The chant spread from one table to another. Gallant looked at her quizzically and was even more surprised when she got up and joined Chui at the bar.

Calls came from every corner, requesting a half dozen of their favorite songs.

Midshipmen were seated at various tables around the room, with local patrons choking the bar and surrounding area. The room fell stone silent as soon as she started to sing. She had their full attention. Within moments they were spellbound.

Kelsey's lovely voice suited the sweet melody,

though the lyrics told a melancholy story of passion and farewell. The audience sat spellbound as she sang several numbers, then returned to her table amid a storm of applause.

"You were marvelous," said Gallant, reaching out to squeeze her hand in admiration.

"Thank you," she said, blushing as if his praise was more meaningful.

Chui continued to play, and several couples got up to dance.

Red nodded at Kelsey while staring at Gallant as if trying to convey some vital information.

Gallant looked blankly at him, but before he could figure out what message Red was sending, Neumann appeared and asked Kelsey to dance. With the barest glance at Gallant, she stood up and took Neumann's hand. He led her onto the dance floor as Chui began to play a slow, romantic melody.

Kelsey nestled comfortably into his arms. Her sweet breath brushed past his cheek; her soft hand gently caressed the nape of his neck.

Kelsey and Neumann were such an attractive couple that they attracted stares from the evening crowd. They seemed indifferent to their momentary celebrity. The joyful people swirled around them in rhythm to the music.

As the slow dance wound down, Chui segued into an old-fashioned cha-cha. As Neumann and Kelsey began the dance, Kelsey turned away, laughing over her shoulder. Neumann followed behind, hands on her waist—one, two, cha, cha, cha. Then they turned around to reverse the direction of the venerable dance. Kelsey had an impish gleam in her eye.

"Which do you prefer: pursuing or being pursued?" Neumann asked with a grin.

Kelsey didn't answer but gave him a coy smile.

Gallant sat rigidly and watched the couple, looking dazed.

Shaking his head in disgust, Red said, "Klutz!"

ENCOUNTER

17

Forty lumbering merchant ships trudged through space in convoy escorted by two destroyers and Fighter Squadron 111. The destroyers intended to make the entire journey from Jupiter to Mars. The fighters were scheduled to tag along for only six days. They were deployed in a lattice radar formation to detect converging asteroids and any alien ships that wandered into their path. As the ships advanced, the density of the asteroid field and the level of danger increased.

Gallant was surprised at how relaxed he felt in his Eagle. His mind felt comfortable with the control systems, adjusting the trim and thrust vector until the ship almost purred. Kelsey monitored obstacles in their flight path and updated the astrogation computer. Gallant adapted the Eagle's flight path for each degree change.

Occasionally, the task force commander altered

the convoy's course to avoid denser asteroid concentrations. Kelsey calculated a new course to maintain their position in the lattice.

We work well together.

Kelsey said, "Caine seems to have found a clever solution to his dilemma."

"You're right," said Gallant. "He plans on having it both ways."

"But will it work?" she asked. Seated tandem with him, she had to raise her voice for Gallant to hear her over the thrumming of the engines.

"It should. By the time we rendezvous with *Dauntless* and *Devastator*, the merchantmen will be deep in the asteroid belt. After that, the convoy will be fine the rest of the way to Mars with the battlecruisers and destroyers. Then the squadron will hotfoot it back to Jupiter before the alien fleet gets there."

"That's cutting things close. I don't want to miss all the action," said Kelsey.

"Don't worry. We won't."

The convoy continued for over three days, Kelsey and Gallant alternating taking naps. While Gallant slept, Kelsey flew the ship using the manual controls. Gallant was impressed with how adept she was at making delicate corrections with such crude instruments.

But then the plan changed.

Gallant had just resumed control of the ship after a nap when Neumann's voice came over the radio. "Gallant, the *Stella Bordeaux* has suffered a fire and internal explosion and needs to repair her engines. Therefore, you are to drop out of formation to provide escort, assist in repairs for three days, and then return to *Repulse* at maximum acceleration. Under no circumstances are you to fail to rendezvous in three days."

"Aye, aye, sir," responded Gallant. He banked his Eagle and positioned it adjacent to the ailing merchantman.

Neumann singled me out.

He cut off the radio and said aloud, "Now we have to play nursemaid."

"Don't pout. It's only for a few days," said Kelsey as they watched the convoy diminish into a distant point of light. "Think of it as an independent command, an opportunity to excel!"

Trust Kelsey to find the silver lining.

He contacted Captain Edward Dawson on *Stella Bordeaux* and asked to be briefed.

Dawson explained, "We had a fire in the reactor compartment. The resulting explosion breached the hull across both the engine room and the reactor compartment. It produced a serious radioactive gas leak as well. We got the fire out and patched the engine room but couldn't enter the reactor compartment with the reactor still hot. So that part of the hull breach will need to be sealed externally."

Gallant said, "Request permission to board *Stella Bordeaux* to visually inspect the damage and decide how best to seal the hull."

"Permission granted—with appreciation."

Gallant looped around the ship to scan the hull then flew into dock with the *Stella Bordeaux*.

Before entering the damaged compartment, Kelsey and Gallant put on their shielded suits.

Gallant checked the reactor compartment pressure. He was sure it read near the normal range when he first arrived, but now the engine room showed a dramatic pressure drop. All the connected compartments were showing abnormally low pressure. The air loss was critical but worse; the differential pressure threatened to rupture the valve seals. That could cause a reactor-core meltdown.

In the meantime, *Stella Bordeaux* remained adrift, an easy target for any hostile ship.

Dawson said, "We're making satisfactory progress on the internal repairs, but I have no one who can do the external repairs. Can you help with that?"

"I've had training in external hull patching," replied Kelsey.

"No, I'll do the spacewalk. Then, the Eagle's AI can guide me through the repairs," said Gallant.

Kelsey leaned in toward Gallant and snapped, "When we're aboard the Eagle, you're the command pilot, and you give the orders. When we're not, I'm senior. My call."

She's serious.

She added quietly, "I'll do the external repairs. Then, you return to the Eagle and use the lasers to keep meteorites from poking holes in me. Clear?"

There was a long moment of brittle tension before Gallant said, "Perfectly."

After collecting the needed materials from ship supplies, Kelsey donned a spacesuit and made her way to the airlock. The jetpack got her to the leak site quickly, and the repairs seemed to go well at first.

But after a half-hour of work, she keyed the suit's intercom and said, "Captain Dawson, the available materials are not up to our needs. I'm afraid these makeshift patches may not last."

"I understand," said Dawson.

As he watched from the Eagle, Gallant felt a vague uneasiness. He was relieved when Kelsey returned safely to the Eagle.

Finally, they were able to restart the reactor at low power. Soon, the ship was limping on one engine, still leaking, although the atmosphere loss had decreased dramatically.

Back in her astrogator's seat, Kelsey suddenly said, "I'm getting a faint radar signature from a ship at the edge of the asteroid field, heading this way."

Gallant looked at the display. It showed a small alien saucer that could outgun the freighter and his fighter.

Opening a communications channel to Dawson, he said, "*Stella Bordeaux*, we have an alien ship on radar. No indication yet that it's currently tracking us, though it may have seen us earlier. Possibly they lost sight of us among the asteroids. Dawson, what would happen if we dumped your cargo of volatile fuel and fired a missile into it?"

For a moment, Dawson didn't respond. Then, a broad smile spread across his face. "We'd give them one heck of a headache!"

"Right. Captain Dawson, plot the saucer's best course toward us and begin discharging the cargo in that direction. When I tell you—start broadcasting on the radio."

Gallant maneuvered the Eagle behind a planetoid to avoid detection and watched the saucer on the display screen. Then, when it was clear the trajectory would take the saucer through the discharged fuel, he contacted *Stella Bordeaux* again.

"Captain, come to all stop and start transmitting."

"We're broadcasting."

The saucer responded to the transmission, changing course to head directly for the *Stella Bordeaux*. Gallant watched as it approached. He calculated its progress toward the fuel while keeping his Eagle behind the planetoid. He was concerned that the fuel was dispersing too quickly.

How long should I wait to fire? What if the saucer detects the fuel and avoids it? Will the dispersed fuel be enough?

"Mr. Gallant, the leak rate in the reactor compartment is increasing again and approaching the danger point. So, we have to reinforce that new seal!"

"Stand by, Captain Dawson," responded Gallant, his eyes fixed on the display.

Just before the saucer reached the fuel, it changed course, aiming to skim past the edge of the spill.

They saw it! Now or never.

The two missiles created an impressive explosion. Although the saucer wasn't caught up in the initial blast, it spun out of control straight into a large asteroid.

The collision demolished the alien craft, leaving nothing but debris. Gallant heaved a sigh of relief, and Kelsey let out a whoop.

"Good work, Henry!"

"Thanks! I'm glad they took the bait. I wouldn't want to go head-to-head with one of those saucers."

Dawson radioed, "Great job! That saucer had me worried. You guys are amazing."

"Thanks, Captain," said Gallant.

"But we still need to take care of this leak," said Dawson. "The damaged area is leaking again. Can Midshipman Mitchel come back over and reseal the breach?"

"Kelsey, would you mind?" asked Gallant, mindful of their earlier conversation.

"I'd be delighted," she responded cheerfully.

Gallant brought his Eagle into a stationary orbit next to the *Stella Bordeaux,* and Kelsey donned her gear and jetted to the damaged area. The work was progressing well when Gallant interrupted her.

"We've got trouble. I have a new contact."

Another alien destroyer popped up from behind a massive asteroid. It was a million kilometers away.

A second Titan destroyer so near doesn't make sense.

A lump formed in Gallant's throat. They'll be in range in a matter of minutes."

Kelsey's a sitting duck.

Throwing caution to the wind, Gallant did the first thing he could think of—powered his Eagle to maximum acceleration and headed toward the saucer.

Immediately the alien fired two anti-ship missiles at the Eagle.

He barely had time to feel relieved before they sent two missiles at him.

He fired two antimissiles, sensing their response through the neural interface.

As the AMM-3 Mongooses flushed from their racks, he felt rather than heard their soundless *swoosh* into the vacuum of space.

They surged to maximum acceleration within seconds, locking on to their target. Then, they tracked them through a complex algorithm based on emissions data, direction, and velocity.

The Titan missiles raced toward Gallant's Eagle. They recognized the approaching Mongoose antimissile as a threat and began countermeasures. They released decoys and conducted evasive maneuvers.

Gallant felt the mental strain as his AI system worked to differentiate its true target and home in on it.

Following the Mongoose flight path in his mind, he scored a direct hit on the first Titan missile, destroying it well out of range of the Eagle. Unfortunately, the second missile exploded seconds later.

Before the destroyer could reload its forward

missile launchers, Gallant fired a missile at the saucer's underbelly. He guessed that was the location of its propulsion. If right, his small missiles could inflict significant damage. Otherwise, he was in deep trouble.

He continued to fire without regard for the saucer's missiles, which bore down on him rapidly. He fired laser blasts at them but spent more effort avoiding them with his flying ability.

Gallant was startled when the saucer suddenly broke off its attack. He wondered whether the Titans feared a kamikaze attack, or his missiles had done enough damage that they'd had enough.

Gallant took several deep breaths to return his adrenaline level to normal. He then turned back to *Stella Bordeaux.*

"That was quite a performance!" said Kelsey over her radio. "I never saw anything like that in the tactical manual."

Gallant asked, "Are you OK?"

"I'm fine. I need a little more time to finish these repairs. But we should have *Stella Bordeaux* running and clear out of this area soon."

"Good. I don't think that the Titan ship will be back. At least, I hope not," he said.

"Well, Mr. Gallant, if you're done gallivanting through space, I'd like to get back aboard my ship as soon as I'm through this repair."

A TEST OF WILLS

18

T en uneasy days after the first radar sighting of the Titan Fleet, Captain Caine led the *Repulse* and a small but steadfast band of ships toward the aliens. Captains Rook of the *Renown*, Minford of the *Remarkable*, and Waller of the *Retribution* followed in a column. A column of five destroyers flanked the battlecruisers. Their men were at battle stations, weapons at the ready, fully confident they would prevail.

On the hangar deck of the *Repulse*, Gallant watched the refueling, rearming, and pre-flight checks being completed on his Eagle. Kelsey sat nearby, arms folded, eyes closed. Nearly four hours had passed since they had returned from their solo escort mission. Bone tired, they had tried to nap but failed. The rest of Squadron 111 had returned earlier and was already rested and prepped.

Making his way through the bustling crowd of

technicians, Chief Benjamin Howard strolled toward Gallant. He extended his hand and said, "Henry, I'm glad I caught you. I wanted to wish you Godspeed."

"Thanks," said Gallant shaking his hand. "Good luck, Benjamin."

They held their grip for a long moment. They sensed that the life they knew was about to change. All too quickly, however, Howard left to take his station in the communications shack while Gallant got aboard his fighter.

Gallant's AI console revealed a mesmerizing scene of the two approaching fleets. Recon drones that had been sent hours before were providing detailed information. It appeared that the Titans were targeting Ganymede and were approaching in three different formations.

Like an octopus, the aliens extended their tentacles toward their prey. Each of the three threatening appendages pointed toward a UP target. They acted in concert to threaten the Jupiter frontier.

The first Titan tentacle was the main battle fleet, about thirty light-seconds ahead of the assault force. It was arranged in an ellipsoid formation as it approached the UP fleet. There was a large outer screen of destroyers with two dozen cruisers inside the perimeter.

The outer screen formed a quilt-like arrangement. Each patch in the quilt was made up of a group of a dozen Titan destroyers arranged in a simple geometric form. They were positioned in three dimensions with three ship triangles at each corner of a square. The outer screen, which consisted of 144 ships, gave the overall appearance of a single solid object.

The Titans had the advantage of being higher up in Jupiter and solar gravity wells. They could withhold their attack until they felt ready, thanks to the orbital dynamics of the planets and suns. They were on a sunward course that would intercept the Jupiter Fleet.

The second formation consisted of twenty-four ships with multiple large shuttles attached. They had small weapons profiles and appeared to be assault transports. Their course targeted Ganymede's central settlement communities. These included Kendra, home to over thirty thousand colonists.

The third formation, made up of another twenty-four destroyers, acted as a covering force for the transports.

It was a moot question to ask how large the alien ground-assault force was. The only military presence on Ganymede was the Seventh Marine Regiment of 1800 men with a few armored vehicles and tanks. The contents of twenty-four assault transports would outmatch them. Such overwhelming strength could only be defeated from space before enemy troops landed on the moon.

Caine sat in his chair on the bridge of the *Repulse*, broadcasting to the aliens on all available channels. Finally, he demanded, "Ships approaching Jupiter Station, identify yourselves."

He repeated this several times before . . .

Then he added, "All fighters deploy in close support formation."

Caine broadcast a video message to the fleet.

"Officers and crew of the Jupiter Fleet, we are faced with a grave threat. The aliens have assembled a powerful force. They intend to attack our settlements. As much as I would like to destroy the assault force, we must first confront their main battle fleet. Their arrangement prevents us from passing through their battle fleet without being annihilated. Therefore, the marine garrison on Ganymede, the research lab, and the Jupiter Station must defend themselves until we have dealt with the Titan's main body.

"The enemy's capabilities and tactics are unfamiliar, but we will learn fast. Their motivation is unknown, but ours is clear. The fate of over three hundred fifty thousand colonists—men, women, and children—rests in our hands. Many of you have family and friends among them. I am certain that each of you will do whatever is necessary to protect them and defeat this enemy. Godspeed."

The fleets approached each other rapidly.

The four large battlecruisers launched their fighters. A total of forty-eight fighters moved in a column, parallel with the five destroyers, to starboard. Caine sent half of his fighter force to fly high cover. The rest of the fighters would remain for close antimissile support.

Gallant flew escort around the battlecruisers.

The Titans' main battle force kept approaching in a tight formation.

The alien's movements were precise, and Gallant wondered whether sentient beings crewed the ships or if they were automated.

The order came, "Flight 4, maintain close support on *Repulse's* forward starboard quarter."

Gallant began visualizing the planets, moons, and nearby ships and their motion. The presence of the many vessels caused him to strain to distinguish distinct patterns. He wondered how the other pilots did it. When he tried to concentrate on the alien formations, he could first see a giant blur of overlapping images. Then, slowly, he could distinguish individual Titan ships and their trajectories.

When the fleets were at a separation of seven light seconds, the aliens began firing missiles. Their flight time would be sixty-four seconds to target.

Gallant noticed that the nuclear-tipped missiles traveled in close-packed groups.

The armored ships with force shields could minimize the blast effects by using acceleration and distance. Ships moving fast were near the explosion for only a tiny fraction of a second. Most of the blast dissipated into empty space. A missile could severely damage the ship's hull plates. Direct hits could penetrate a ship's shields and tear open the hull. Near misses could contribute to the damage ships suffered by weakening shields and armor over time.

The Titan's close-packed missile launch indicated that they were targeting a small area with a high density of warheads. As a result, they were expecting some direct hits.

The alien fleet of one hundred and forty-four destroyers and twenty-four cruisers faced the UP's nine ships. But they had no small craft comparable to the UP's forty-eight fighters. Previous encounters had shown that UP ships had a slight technological advantage. But the saucers were more maneuverable and had greater acceleration.

Caine ordered a full salvo of Hydra-III missiles fired from the battlecruisers. Smaller missiles were fired from the destroyers. This totaled fifty-two missiles. Sooner than Gallant thought possible, missiles belched from the *Repulse's* bow, and the beginning of a life-and-death struggle began.

The aliens' first missile volley of 384 large and small missiles approached.

The UP fleet deployed countermeasures. Decoys and chaff misdirected more than a third of the incoming weapons.

Then, it was the fighters' turn. They spread like a fan moving through space like sharks hunting for prey. When they acquired a target, they launched their AMM-3 Mongoose antimissile missiles.

Using his neural interface, Gallant was able to visualize each incoming missile. He had a window of only twenty-four seconds to engage them. First, he envisioned the individual rockets but had a problem with the sheer numbers. Slowly and methodically, his mind constructed a comprehensive image of the battlefield. Finally, he had a grand view, including every individual missile and its flight solution. He identified each object with a streak of motion that appeared like a vector arrow illustrating its direction. As his understanding of the dynamic situation improved, he discovered that many of his fellow pilots were shooting at the same targets while ignoring others. It occurred to him that they didn't have as comprehensive an interpretation of the battlefield as he did.

Is it possible with all their vaunted genetic engineering advantages, my Natural talent was superior?

Over the communication channel, Gallant said, "Red, you are targeting incoming missiles that Flight 5 is also targeting. Shift to the next pair to starboard."

"How can you tell?" asked Red.

"Never mind for now. I can."

"Roger."

"Flight One, you are targeting the same missiles as Flight Two. Shift to the next two targets to port," he instructed.

"Roger," the pilot immediately replied.

Next, Gallant started to direct other squadrons.

He said, "Squadron 112, you are overlapping targets with Squadron 113. Therefore, I recommend you shift to targets below the reference plane and let 113 focus on targets above."

He was pleased that his shipmates accepted his instructions. But then he heard Neumann ask, "Can you distinguish individual missiles within such a dense launch at this distance?"

"Yes. I can follow every single alien missile

and extrapolate its full trajectory. Then, with your permission, I'll help direct antimissile launches to optimize our fire," said Gallant.

"Permission granted," said Neumann.

With feedback from Kelsey, Gallant destroyed eight ship-killer missiles. Then, under his direction, his forty-seven fellow pilots took care of one hundred of the remaining projectiles. Then the ship's antimissile batteries took out about another hundred.

Only a few dozen alien missiles detonated near their target, Captain Rook's *Renown*.

The first tremendous shock of explosions accentuated the Jupiter Fleet's grave danger. The nuclear warheads damaged the battlecruiser's forward shield and bow plates considerably. The *Renown's* forward missile compartment was ruptured and rendered useless.

Although the fighters were not as well protected, they accelerated up to five times as fast. In addition, their CMG generated enough torque to let their spacecraft flip end-for-end in seconds. This allowed them to limit their exposure to nuclear blasts. Nevertheless, one of *Renown's* fighters was bracketed and crippled.

We've survived the first blow of the battle.

"That tells us something of their command structure," said Kelsey. "They targeted the *Renown* because they didn't expect our commander to be in the lead ship."

"Good observation," said Gallant.

The flight time of the UP missiles was seventy

seconds. The aliens deployed countermeasures as the UP's fifty-two missiles approached their target. That diverted eleven. Antimissile missiles from the saucers were strewn in the path of the remaining forty-one missiles. Nevertheless, Gallant distinguished a dozen explosions that appeared to disable or destroy three Titan destroyers and two cruisers.

The UP fleet had gotten the better of the first exchange despite its fewer numbers.

If Caine remained on his current course, the enemy could cross his T. It was a long-standing naval convention; crossing the T of one's enemy brought superior firepower to bear. In this tactical dilemma, Caine compromised and swung his column.

Caine ordered, "Hard to port. Come to course 120, azimuth up 10 degrees at 1626."

The range continued to close while all the ships reloaded their missile tubes. The destroyer column remained on Caine's starboard side, which was closer to the Titan fleet.

After a few minutes, the Titans had completed their reloading and launched their second volley of missiles. Then, they changed their course to 330 to close the distance with the UP fleet more quickly.

Caine ordered a further turn, hoping to confuse the incoming missiles, "Hard to starboard, come to course 220, azimuth up 10 degrees, at time 1632. All fighters move to close-in support."

Caine was now moving across the Titan's line of advancement.

"All ships prepare to fire. Fire!" The second UP

salvo was on its way.

The follow-up missile exchange produced similar results. The *Renown* was bruised, and several fighters were destroyed. Several of the Titan destroyers and a cruiser were knocked out. The two fleets continued to close. At 1638, the Jupiter Fleet had traveled nearly half a million kilometers since the start of the action. The two enemy forces were now less than a million kilometers apart, nearly within plasma and laser range.

Captain Waller of the *Retribution* signaled, "Recommend concentrating fire on the damaged ships. So, we could finish them off."

Caine didn't reply but continued to cross the aliens' T just as they reached plasma and laser range.

This move probably saved the Jupiter Fleet. As the distance closed, the Titan plasma fire proved devastating, and the UP ships writhed from the onslaught. The neighboring space was lit up with the glow of multiple radiation bursts and reflections. Two UP destroyers were damaged, and the *Remarkable* took a few hits that scorched its port side.

A very confused struggle wore on.

The simultaneous missile strikes left behind a mess of drifting broken ships. The bow of a UP destroyer was blown off.

Caine ordered, "All ships prepare to fire missile salvo. Fire. Hard to port. Come to course 180, azimuth up 10 degrees at 1646."

This bold call turned the UP fleet directly toward the enemy and quickly closed the range. They were following their missiles toward the enemy ships.

The missile flight time was a mere twenty seconds, and it didn't allow the aliens time to deploy decoys or countermeasures. It completely disrupted their organization. Instead of firing a return salvo, the alien ships spent several confused minutes avoiding collisions. A dozen Titan destroyers and several cruisers were destroyed or severely damaged.

The Titans ordered a general attack. Their fleet split into different divisions and attacked independently. The Titan cruisers were forced into repeated evasive actions. This slowed their advance and increased the confusion in the already badly disorganized formation.

Kelsey said, "Look at Ganymede. It's being bombarded. I hope there are enough underground shelters to protect the population. Shuttlecraft were on their way to the surface. Alien ground forces are attacking the marine base."

Gallant thought of Jake's son, Sergeant Bernstein. He said, "It looks like they'll be overrun."

Caine must have been thinking the same thing because Gallant heard him signal the Ganymede troops, "Stand firm. We're coming."

Caine used his current tactical advantage to pass through the Titan battle fleet. It forced them to reverse their course to follow him. This would give him a clear shot at the assault force attacking Ganymede. But he would have to hurry; the assault force's bombardment was wreaking havoc on the moon.

Caine hoped to cut through the Titan formation just in front of the enemy cruisers, isolating some ships in front and taking them out of combat. The plan would allow the fleets to close their distance quickly. It would also bring on a frantic battle by breaking the Titan line. There were a series of individual ship-to-ship fights in which the UP spacecraft would likely prevail. Caine knew his ships had better gunnery and defensive measures. The main drawback of attacking head-on was that as the leading UP ships approached, the Titan ships could direct broadside fire at their bows.

The UP and Titans were now in a jagged, curved line, headed toward each other. The badly damaged UP fleet approached the disorganized Titan formation. The foremost UP ships were under heavy fire from several enemy ships for a considerable time before they could return fire. For many tense minutes, *Repulse* was under fire from the Titan cruisers. Although many shots went astray, others killed and wounded many of her crew.

Caine's force attacked the assault ships. The shuttles in flight were burned to a crisp, and the alien assault force was badly mauled.

However, Jupiter Fleet paid a heavy price for this maneuver. The main Titan battle force launched a missile salvo with devastating effects.

Gallant and his comrades struggled to shoot down the incoming missiles, even as plasma and laser beams cut them apart.

Despite the fighters' best efforts, two destroyers

were badly damaged and fell out of formation. In addition, the *Retribution* was severely damaged and had to reduce acceleration. Nearly half of the fleet's fighters were also destroyed or severely damaged.

"Ken, we're crippled, and we must fall out of formation," reported William Waller of the *Retribution*.

In a desperate gamble to save the battlecruiser, Caine ordered, "All fighters attack enemy forces at close range."

"All squadrons form on 111," ordered Neumann. "Guide on me."

The remaining twenty-six fighters fell into an attack formation. They descended upon the Titan fleet like a pack of wolves—straight into the teeth of the enemy's defenses.

"Flight 4, stay tight," urged Red.

Gallant acknowledged, "I'm with you."

The fighters weaved through the Titan ships, striking their blows. Then, to avoid collisions with the enemy and friendly ships, they shot at targets of opportunity.

The Titan's close-range plasma blasts produced a cataclysm of violence.

Gallant was stunned when Sandy Barrington's fighter took a direct hit. It disintegrated and broke into hundreds of pieces right before his eyes.

Despite the heroic assault, the enemy ships stayed on course. The fighters, however, were decimated by plasma cannons from all sides and had to break off. Less than half returned to the fleet.

As the Titans closed in on *Retribution*, she fought a desperate battle. On her own, against overwhelming odds, she was hit mercilessly with missile after missile. Belching wreckage and air, she staggered bravely onward. Finally, she erupted, and the dying wreck disappeared into a giant fireball.

As the battle ebbed and flowed, the superior number of saucers significantly impacted the UP ships. Unfortunately, the battle was only one hour old, and thousands had already died.

When the afterglow of the *Retribution's* explosion faded, Caine turned his remaining ships to open some distance to the enemy. He commanded, "Hard to starboard. Come to course 090, azimuth up 10 degrees, at 1716."

The Titans changed formation and moved to

open the distance between the fleets. Both sides needed time to regroup.

Fourteen of the Titans' cruisers remained in the center of a screen of forty-eight destroyers—four patches of a dozen destroyers each. Their remaining cruisers and destroyers had been demolished or left as derelicts floating in Jupiter's orbit. The battle now continued at long range.

The remains of the enemy assault force continued to attack Ganymede and bombard the Jupiter Station. Finally, one group split off to attack the colonies on Ganymede.

Caine was forced to keep what remained of the Jupiter Fleet together, leaving Jupiter Station and Ganymede to defend themselves.

Gallant was flying on Gregory's wing when he tracked inbound missiles with a zero-bearing rate.

"Red, incoming. Hard to starboard! Kick it hard!" said Gallant, his stomach reeling.

"Roger!" The explosion rocked both ships.

Red's Eagle took substantial damage from the near miss.

"Henry, my Eagle's hit, one engine blown. I'm burned down the side of my body, and I think my arm is broken. I'm heading for the barn. You're on your own now." Then, a moment later, he added, "Good luck."

Gallant covered Red's retreat as he left formation and limped back to the *Repulse.*

Soon, several more fighters were damaged or destroyed. Then another destroyer fell out of formation, badly damaged from direct missile hits.

Several fighters tried to extend their antimissile screen to cover the damaged ships, but they became easy targets for the saucers.

Caine ordered the fleet to maneuver to better support the damaged ships, but the aliens attacked in group formations of a dozen ships at a time. Finally, they fired their missiles in salvos and quickly withdrew.

Gallant fired his antimissiles at incoming missiles and his lasers at nearby saucers. All the time, he maintained his relative velocity alongside the *Repulse* by accelerating in a tight spiral. In addition, he constantly offered target information to the other pilots who were eager for his input.

The UP ships had no chance to fall back for repairs, and with Jupiter Station under attack, they had no haven. They could only keep fighting. Although an increasing number of escape pods drifted among the battle wreckage, no one was available to rescue them.

By now, Jupiter Station and Ganymede were embroiled in combat. Fortunately, the cloaked laboratory had the FASER cannon primed and ready to disintegrate any saucers in range. Unfortunately, the lab had only had time to build a few MASS mines, but those were deployed near Jupiter Station.

The aliens concentrated their attack on the battlecruisers as they moved away beyond missile range.

Although the outcome of the battle was still

in doubt, the battlecruisers had taken considerable damage.

A saucer that had been hit by missile fire drifted toward Gallant's fighter in a slow spin. It looked reasonably intact but didn't respond to his laser blasts. His finger hovered over the missile firing button as he considered his options.

This may be a rare opportunity.

"Kelsey, I'm going to board that saucer and see what's inside."

"No, no, no, Henry! Is that . . . even possible in the middle of all this chaos?"

"It's an opportunity we can't afford to pass up."

She said nothing for several long seconds. Then her natural curiosity kicked in. She calculated the course to dock and matched the saucer's velocity, course, and orientation.

"Kelsey, use the lasers to cover my spacewalk, but I have no way of knowing whether the ship's crew will offer any resistance," said Gallant. "If things go badly, I want you to break off."

"I'll tell *Repulse* what you're attempting. Maybe they can provide covering fire if needed," she said.

"Great idea. I'll send a video feed from my suit comm pin. That way, *Repulse* can follow my progress and record the encounter for intelligence analysis."

Ignoring the aftermath of the violent battle that lingered around him, Gallant sealed his armored suit, strapped on his gun, and exited the fighter through his overhead airlock. Short bursts of his jetpack directed him along the surface of the fighter as he looked for a way.

Gallant increased the filter setting of his visor to protect him from deadly radiation. Micrometers pelleted him. They were hundreds of times faster than high-velocity rifle bullets. One tear in the pressurized suit and his blood would boil, bursting him like a toy balloon within seconds.

He heard Kelsey call *Repulse*. "We're under direct fire! We need immediate support!" A look over his shoulder confirmed that another saucer was headed toward him, spurting laser blasts.

She's worried about me.

A distorted answer came from the OOD on *Repulse*. "We can fire ... at ... but with the radiation interference hitting . . . would be pure luck."

"If you fire a missile with external laser guidance, I can paint the target with my fighter's laser," responded Kelsey, her voice steady.

"Will do; stand by."

Repulse fired, and Kelsey lit up the target saucer. Then, with a satisfying explosion, the alien ship disintegrated into a shower of debris.

"Fantastic!" exclaimed Gallant. "Thanks, *Repulse*! And you too, Kelsey!"

He turned his attention back to the saucer in front of him. Working his way around the saucer, he finally found a massive hole in the hull.

Just inside the hull breach, he froze in shock. Several alien crew members floated around the compartment. Their ruptured bodies were grotesque in the flickering light. He had to tear his eyes away from their strange, gray-purple faces and force himself to move past them. Then, handgun at the ready, he crept toward the next compartment.

Gallant guessed that a radial corridor would lead him to the bridge in the saucer's center. The reactor compartment and engine rooms were likely along the outer circumference.

He moved forward step by step, leading with the gun in his right hand, sweeping it back and forth and alert to any flicker of motion. On the way, he passed several more alien bodies. They were mangled from explosions and fire. Many had not even made it into their protective suits before the saucer depressurized. He paused to examine one of the bodies. They were thin, about two meters, with long limbs and slender appendages. They had odd leathery skin, bare of any hair or markings. He stared in fascination at the eyes—violet and cobalt, even in death shining like iridescent moons.

He picked up one of the aliens' weapons. The highly polished barrel made it look like an assault weapon, possibly a high-temperature plasma gun. He cast it aside and kept going.

Once on the bridge, he searched for life among the crew through the rubble but found none. He scanned the bridge controls. It was an impossible task, and he was unwilling to risk manipulating anything.

A grating noise made him turn to see the hatch to the bridge swing open. Two aliens entered the compartment, as surprised as he was by the intrusion.

With all the bravado he could muster, Gallant

thrust himself forward, firing at them in quick succession. As they crumpled to the floor, his hands shook, and he almost dropped his weapon. Instead, he turned his back on their dead bodies, pushing aside the dark thoughts that flooded his mind, and focused his attention on the control console.

He was examining what he hoped was the central processing unit when another Titan suddenly appeared and fired at him. He jumped back in alarm and lost his balance, and the fall saved his life. The plasma blast only grazed Gallant's left arm. His reflexes brought his gun up first as he rolled, and the alien's face evaporated.

He sat on the floor for a moment, breathing hard. His armored suit automatically sealed itself. It activated the suit's emergency medical response unit and released an antiseptic onto his wound. He bit his lip against the searing pain, even with the automatic analgesic. He forced himself to stand up to keep from succumbing to shock.

After a few minutes, the medications took effect, and he assessed his options and addressed the alien systems around him.

He took a flask from his equipment belt and collected tissue samples from the alien bodies. Then using a metal bar from the debris, he pried out what he guessed was a vital piece of equipment—a cylindrical mechanism a meter long, pointed on both ends and bristling with integrated circuits. The device looked extremely complex and bore all an AI system's earmarks.

His injured arm made the trip back to his fighter difficult. Once there, however, he remained outwardly impassive and had to ask for help.

Kelsey grabbed him and helped him aboard. Then she shoved the mechanism into a locker below the pilot's seat.

Biting his lip, he said, "Contact *Repulse.* That thing is important alien technology. UP Command will want to see it right away."

By now, the battle was in a lull while the two sides regrouped, but the UP fleet was in trouble. Nearly all the fighters were destroyed or badly damaged. The battlecruisers were all in need of repair and low on missiles. Recognizing the critical importance of what Gallant had recovered, Captain Caine responded over a secure channel. He asked about the alien technology.

Neumann said, "Captain, let me take the equipment to Ganymede Lab for study." Caine responded, "Ganymede isn't safe. It'll have to go to Mars."

Gallant said, "Let me take it, Captain."

Neumann interjected, "No, Captain, I should take it. Mars is at the very edge of the Eagles' range, and the asteroids are inundated with aliens. I'm senior and the better pilot."

Caine was quiet, deliberating.

Gallant took a deep breath.

For months, I've let Neumann intimidate me with his genetic advantages—that stops today.

"Sir," said Gallant. "I'm the one who took the

risk and captured that technology. I'm the one who can get it to Mars."

Caine said thoughtfully, "You continue to surprise me, Mr. Gallant."

He paused and weighed the options, then said briskly, "Mr. Gallant, break off from the battle and take the alien unit to a UP base. Remember, you have limited fuel and environmental capabilities. Flight 3, you will provide cover and escort Midshipman Gallant out of the immediate combat area. The battlecruisers will re-engage the enemy fleet to keep them occupied as long as possible. Good luck!"

Gallant, Neumann, and Chui moved into formation and turned toward Mars. Weaving between damaged ships, it looked like the three fighters would get away. But then, two saucers broke away from the main engagement and sped after them.

"OK, this is on us, Chui," said Neumann. "Gallant, stay on course. We've got your back. Don't let us down!"

He and Chui turned and flew head-on toward the two saucers.

"Roger, and Godspeed," muttered Gallant, his throat dry, as his Eagle headed off alone.

He watched Flight 3's Eagles for as long as he could until they suddenly vanished in a massive explosion at the edge of his instrument range.

"Oh, Henry," Kelsey gasped.

Taking a deep breath, Gallant somberly focused his attention on the vastness of space before him.

With grim determination, he said, "Let's get

this equipment to Mars."

THE LAST STARFIGHTER

19

Midshipman Henry Gallant aimed his Eagle toward the sun.

The star's radiance thrust golden barbs into the surrounding coal-black space. Rocks and dust in the asteroid belt twinkled as they moved across its face. The unwelcoming asteroid belt with its uncountable deluge of rocks and debris was strewn before him. The aftermath of a ferocious battle fought in the shadow of Jupiter was scattered behind him.

He narrowed his eyes as he glanced over his shoulder and watched Kelsey adjust the visual display of the ship's long-range telescope. He could still distinguish the derelict and broken ships of the Jupiter Fleet in the distance. He tried not to dwell on the ferocious battle, although he knew the colonies and facilities on the frontier might even now be at the mercy of the Titans. He felt torn between the guilt of leaving his shipmates behind and the need to get critical alien technology to Mars for analysis.

As he stripped off his armored suit, pain shot up his arm from the plasma wound. With its own circulatory system of medical fluids interwoven within the various layers. It was like the body's arteries.

Despite the spasms, he remained stone-faced while he cut away the burned sleeve of the underlying pressure suit. This exposed his seared forearm. His flesh was scorched and blackened from the shoulder down to his wrist.

Kelsey squirmed forward to his seat.

"Oh, Henry," she grimaced.

She fought down her revulsion and set about cleaning the charred area.

When a moan escaped his lips, she glanced at his face and said, "Let me give you another shot for the pain." She loaded a needle with a powerful anesthetic and injected it into the tender skin. Slathering more antiseptic over the wound, she dabbed a healing gel on top before bandaging the arm.

Her forehead creased with a concerned look as she gazed into Gallant's face.

"How's that?" she asked.

After a deep breath, he sneered at his weakness. "Better, much better."

Good thing that alien's aim wasn't better.

He opened the food storage cabinet and pulled

out a synthetic supplement, splitting the contents between them. Both knew they had millions of kilometers to go before they could find any sanctuary, and he expected they would be on short rations for the trip. As they munched on the unappetizing foodstuff, he checked the Eagle's life-support system. He asked the AI system to evaluate their supplies.

"I think we should reduce power consumption to optimize our flight time," he said.

"Agreed," said Kelsey. She adjusted the life-support system to hold oxygen at 80 percent of normal and decrease the operating capacity of the carbon dioxide. "That should extend our overall life-support capabilities by a couple of days."

Gallant also optimized course to conserve fuel.

"We need a fuel-efficient plan for traversing the asteroid belt while avoiding Titan scout ships. When we were escorting the *Stella Bordeaux*, we saw a lot of alien activity throughout the area."

"What did you have in mind?" asked Kelsey, working her way around Gallant's seat back to her own.

"We need to find a trajectory within our resource limitations that provides cover through the asteroid field. And plot a course through the asteroid belt that minimizes fuel consumption."

The AI system displayed several alternatives.

"Am I wrong, or do these paths seem inadequate?" asked Kelsey, a touch of exasperation in her voice.

"This trajectory isn't too bad," Gallant said,

pointing at the display. "It meets our basic parameters for fuel and life-support, although it doesn't keep us particularly well hidden. But they all offer only limited radar stealth."

"How about we zigzag from one large asteroid formation to another in short bursts? Even if the Titans get a couple of quick returns on radar, they won't have anything solid to track. And we can minimize our radar profile when we're in the open. Let me try programming a route," suggested Kelsey.

The adjusted life-support settings changed the familiar hum of his ship, but Gallant concentrated on his display. He had faith in Kelsey's expertise to find a safe course to Mars.

"Look at this, Henry," she said.

He studied the route for a moment, then asked, "Why did you pick this leg here toward Ceres?"

"It's near the center of the asteroid field, and that large cluster of asteroids will provide excellent radar shelter. By moving toward that cluster, we have the best probability of stealth. I've searched my mind for any critical detail I might've overlooked, but this is the best path I could find."

Gallant said, "Let's do it."

Gallant awoke with a start. He lay in the bunk, wondering what had roused him, then realized it was the persistent beeping of the communications center. His heart pounded as he stretched to activate the decoding equipment, then climbed out of the bunk, and into the pilot's seat.

They had a signal from Jupiter Fleet. Gallant almost choked with nervousness and excitement as his mind ran through possible messages. He leaned forward, peering at the screen, and felt Kelsey's breath on his neck as she craned over his shoulder.

He let out a sigh and let his shoulders relax. The message was from Chief Howard. The first words were, "Gregory and Neumann arrived back at Jupiter Station and are recovering at the station hospital." It went on to list the names of crewmen who had not survived the battle. There were so many, too many. Gallant closed his eyes and gave a silent mental salute.

Kelsey squeezed his shoulder. She was doing the same.

A four-line family-gram from Kelsey's family was included, retransmitted from Earth.

She read it aloud, "Everyone here is fine and praying for you. Stay safe. Much love, Mom and Dad."

Gallant felt a twinge of envy.

The rest of the transmission gave an update on the battle. The battlecruisers had been badly damaged but were under repair. The Marines on Ganymede were holding their position near the Titan landing zones. While the aliens hadn't been beaten back, they hadn't advanced any further. It left the conflict in gridlock with neither side strong enough to dislodge the other.

"Do you think it's odd that the Titans aren't following up their attack?" asked Kelsey.

Gallant said, "The entire Titan strategy for this war doesn't make any sense. They attacked Jupiter with a force too small for sustained follow-through. Even if they had succeeded in destroying Jupiter Fleet and occupying Ganymede, they can't withstand a counterattack. Mars Fleet could brush them off Ganymede like so many flies." He thought for a few long seconds, considering. "Playing chess against Red has taught me that the opening moves aren't designed to bring about an immediate, decisive win. They may be setting up a favorable position to gain a more decisive advantage. We're missing something."

***

Jupiter receded in the distance as the Eagle made slow but steady progress through the asteroid field. Occasionally, Gallant and Kelsey shared stories and recalled pleasant events. That helped them form a bond in their isolation, and the normalcy of conversation distracted them from their lost comrades.

At the same time, the physical burden of their environmental conditions became uncomfortable. After several days, the buildup of perspiration made Gallant's pressure suit cling to his skin. He washed and shaved as best as he could in the tiny basin. His bandaged arm hampering him as much as the cramped quarters as he splashed water and cleanser over his face and neck. He yearned for a brisk shower, but that was only available on the distant *Repulse*. His head constantly throbbed from the reduced oxygen and excess carbon dioxide. He imagined that he made quite an unpleasant sight.

But the worst was the slowly healing wound. Fingers twitching at his bandage, he said restlessly, "I've got to do something to stop this itching. It's driving me crazy."

Kelsey said, "Don't you dare touch that bandage. I did a very nice job dressing that wound if I do say so myself, and I don't want you introducing an infection."

Gallant opened the food lockers and pulled out the meal's ration of synthetic food and water. Restricted to two small meals each day, they anticipated each one more than the last. Kelsey joined him in the forward portion of the ship to share the simple meal. It was the only time they could forget their difficult circumstances. But after several days, even the welcomed nourishment was losing its appeal.

Scrunching his face in distaste, Gallant said, "How long have we been out here? These synthetic concentrates already taste like chalk."

Kelsey nodded. "My mouth is watering for a sugary dessert right now."

They remained quiet for a while, salivating over their recollections of better dinners while their appetite drove them to finish their sparse meal.

Navigating through the asteroid field kept them busy. They checked the radar sightings whenever they caught a glimpse of other ships. Once they learned to disregard the incessant collision warnings, they enjoyed the expanse. And they never tired of gazing at the ultimate beauty of space outside their viewing ports.

With nothing and no one else to distract them, it seemed natural to share more and more of their personal stories as the days slid by.

Kelsey chatted about her home life and friends on *Repulse*. Gallant learned to listen without envy about her comfortable family background. In turn, he spoke of his own experience growing up as a colonist on Mars.

As he became less self-conscious, he told her of his ambitions and daydreams, and she listened without judgment or skepticism. Her calm voice soothed his tensions. When she slept, he missed her company despite her nearness.

Sometimes words so crowded his thoughts that his mouth couldn't let them out fast enough, and other times he hardly knew what he wanted to say to her. On occasion, she halted their conversation abruptly, as if she wanted to add something important but couldn't find the right words. At those moments, they looked at each other, waiting and hoping for inspiration.

They talked about books they had read and poems they enjoyed. But their conversations always turned to the same subject—their shipmates and the feelings of loss.

"How about examining the Titans' AI CPU unit?" he suggested one day as a distraction from the monotony.

Kelsey nodded enthusiastically.

He opened the storage locker and pulled out the alien device, turning it over to examine it from every angle. Together they scrutinized the connection fittings, the exposed circuit chips, and even the material itself.

"I took this from the Titan ship because it was integrated into the main Titan computer. My guess was that it was part of the AI CPU, but it's quite different from anything I've seen before. What do you think?"

"I've seen some schematics for our own AI equipment. Why don't we look at the Eagle's AI interface unit and compare them?"

"The aliens must work collectively to fly the Titan destroyers. I think the AI unit sends commands to the aliens, and vice versa. A lot of aliens would need to connect through the neural interface at the same time to manipulate all the ship controls in a coordinated fashion."

"Do you mean they might have some limited telepathy?"

"Well, suppose the Titans were partially telepathic. They could communicate among themselves, using the AI as a supplement."

"This is too complex for us to evaluate on our own," said Kelsey with a frown.

SCARE

20

As uncounted hours passed, and the Eagle lurched its way through the debris, Gallant's appreciation for Kelsey grew. Her course calculations got them through the areas of highest meteor density without a scratch. They had fallen into a comfortable rhythm. They alternated six-hour watch cycles, followed by hours of equipment repair or whatever sleep they could squeeze in.

He didn't recognize it at first, but Gallant's headaches from the neural interface had gradually disappeared. On the other hand, the low oxygen and high carbon dioxide atmosphere made his head throb, and he was constantly gasping for breath. But his biggest worry was the fuel and food supply. Every time he looked in the food locker, he shook his head, trying to figure out how to squeeze his resources a little further.

Each cycle, when he woke, he smoothed his

crumpled uniform and performed isometric exercises in the tiny compartment. While the limited space was a source of irritation, it did not dampen his spirits.

Absentmindedly, he tapped his finger against the cup of stim-coffee and took a few sips along with a bite of the food. He asked, "What are the chances of us stopping at one of the mining colonies somewhere in the belt to get some additional fuel and supplies?"

Kelsey didn't reply right away. She gazed out the viewing port, lost in thought. Finally, she said, "Even if we found a mining facility on our path, odds are they wouldn't have many resources to spare. Besides, prolonging our transit will increase the chances of running into a Titan scout ship."

She pulled up their flight trajectory on the display and compared it to the AI system's colony information. She said, "Unfortunately, this sector is very sparsely settled. One mining colony on the far side of Ceres has some possibilities. It's very small, but not far off our route. It wouldn't cause much of a delay."

Gallant looked at the chart. "Perhaps we'll look in as we pass."

Suddenly distracted, he said, "Kelsey, look at the pattern of Titan ships scouting the area. There's a distinct concentration as we approach Ceres. Even though we've been keeping our radar profile small, it is possible that the Titans caught on to us and are sending extra ships? I can't imagine a lone fighter limping through the asteroid belt would be worth their time."

Kelsey said, "Something strange is going on. Perhaps they're looking for convoys to disrupt our commerce. But why wouldn't they be concentrating on Jupiter?"

Several days later, the Eagle reached the dwarf planet Ceres. It was surrounded by a family cluster, thousands of asteroids in all sizes and shapes. The high density of asteroids created a nest of rocky obstacles that made navigation challenging. But the obscured radar returns, made it the perfect sanctuary.

But as the Eagle cleared a radar shadow, the viewscreen lit up with a brilliant display.

Gallant and Kelsey gaped at the vast armada that had appeared before them. Rows of Titan ships orbited the Ceres cluster—destroyers, cruisers, and battlecruisers. Space stations, fortresses, and methane-production facilities were distributed around the asteroid cluster.

Gallant said, "AI, record data on all Titan forces, installations, and activity in the area." Kelsey scrambled to keep up with the information being collected, adding comments for everything she could. She looked at Gallant with wide eyes and said, "Ironic, isn't it? Leapfrogging from cluster to cluster, and we just happened upon the best hiding place in the asteroid belt, where the Titans built a secret base!"

Gallant maneuvered the Eagle to a less exposed position. The ship bobbed and weaved between asteroids to keep out of the Titans' sensors while they collected information.

The aggregate was staggering—two hundred eighty-eight destroyers, seventy-two cruisers, twelve battlecruisers, three space stations, and six fortresses. He did a quick calculation in his head. The Mars Fleet consisted of two hundred destroyers, sixty cruisers, and twenty-four battlecruisers.

He said, "Mars Fleet should be powerful enough to deal with this armada."

Kelsey said thoughtfully, "UP is likely planning to send a relief force to Jupiter Station soon. That would take ships away from the defense of Mars. Then this Titan armada would be a scary threat."

HIDING

21

Gallant readjusted his neural interface, noting the positions of every ship in the vicinity. The rapid maneuvers required for safe navigation took his full concentration. Kelsey fed him course changes. He had little opportunity to look for their next hiding place.

They kept to the sunward side of Ceres, which offered better concealment. He was relieved when the scanners indicated a crevasse on the surface of a nearby large asteroid. He landed the Eagle with a bump and disengaged from the neural interface, rubbing his dry eyes, stiff neck, and pounding forehead in turn.

"We need to get out of here," said Kelsey.

Gallant nodded

We'll find a way.

But before he could answer, everything changed.

"Ping . . . Ping . . . Ping . . . Ping . . ." They had been discovered.

There was nothing subtle about the situation they found themselves in. They had to scramble out of the crevasse and get moving. They were fighting for their lives; outgunned a million to one.

As Gallant began evasive maneuvers, he prepared but did not transmit a message to warn Mars. He would transmit the message only if the Eagle was about to be destroyed. It was a tough choice, but the only one he could reasonably make. To transmit immediately would give away their exact position.

After a minute, Kelsey leaned forward and touched his shoulder and said calmly, "They've found us. I thought this was a tight spot. I have no doubt now."

She indicated toward two dangerous cruisers angling their way.

Gallant stopped and scanned their surroundings. He saw two more ships approaching.

"Do you think there's an escape route?"

"Possibly. Keep moving," she said.

His survival instincts taking over. He quickened the pace.

He felt, rather than saw, Kelsey scanned the area once more. Her grip on his shoulder tightened.

A dozen potential escape paths flew through his mind—each as impractical as the next.

Stay with the rocks, run for it, broadcast a final distress message. Would any of those options stop determined aliens?

He thrust aside the gloomy possibilities. What he knew was he had to think clearly.

The Eagle weaved past obstacles.

He said, "We've stirred them up, but they're not sure how to make their move."

"Yeah."

"There are two more ahead," she said. "Can you see them? Those following are coming closer, the ones across the area had stopped and were waiting. And there," she said, pointing out another ship.

"They're closing the net," he said.

"Oh, look. The first two are coming this way.

"We'll have to vanish behind some rocks."

He gazed at her eyes and saw no fear, only a firm resolve.

She nodded once. "Let's go."

The Eagle accelerated at maximum thrust.

The aliens swarmed.

But Gallant and Kelsey eluded the first pair of attackers. They ducked behind another rock.

"There they are!" she cried.

Gallant performed a radical turn that maximized the gyroscopic action of the Eagle.

Is anyone following?

They tried to make a quick exit, but as they skittered away from one Titan destroyer, their path was blocked by a large convoy. He realized they were about to be hemmed in by scores of transports and shuttles, escorted by several destroyers and cruisers. The convoy's course posed the very real danger of cutting off their path of escape.

Kelsey said, "Henry, more destroyers to port."

Gallant couldn't spare a thought to respond. He thrust the Eagle forward at full acceleration, his eyes locked on the radar scope as he searched for an escape route. The Eagle rolled to 30 degrees as he wrenched her to starboard.

Cruisers on both sides flicked in and out of view on his radar display, and he hoped the same was true of his ship.

Even if they can't get a lock, they can still track our trajectory.

He concentrated on sudden, erratic moves, using the neural interface to create a map of ships and asteroids. He adjusted the Eagle's actions accordingly. The AI effortlessly translated his thoughts into movement.

Port. Down.

They were hemmed in, surrounded by a net of ships and asteroids.

Starboard. Down. Up.

He sensed rather than saw one narrow avenue of escape, but the destroyers were fast enough to close the gap if they realized where he was heading.

Port. Starboard. Create confusion.

His mind in overdrive, he turned the Eagle directly toward the convoy. Scattering the ships would disrupt their flight patterns and make it harder for the destroyers to either track or fire at him.

Hard to port.

He was confident that he could use his mind's eye view to preserve his position relative to the enemy ships.

Several missiles headed in his direction. Gallant fired his remaining antimissiles. He imagined he heard the SWOOSH as the missiles shot out of the Eagle's tubes.

Hard to starboard. Harder!

He hurtled toward the gap.

"Missiles approaching starboard," reported Kelsey.

Gallant was too focused on flying to reply. The Titan destroyers to port were closing in, pulling the net tighter around him. At the same time, he saw the convoy scrambling to get out of the way.

A cruiser spat yet another missile toward him. The warhead detonated off to starboard, and he felt the Eagle lurch and shudder, but it held steady on course.

Close, but no damage. Hard to starboard, up five degrees.

The Eagle leaped into the midst of the convoy and shot over the bow of a ship, almost clipping the edge.

The number of ships so close together made an effective Titan attack almost impossible. The convoy started to scatter as he darted among the cluster of ships. Confusion spread as both the merchantman and the combat ships tried to avoid running into his Eagle, each other, and the asteroids. A grin flashed across his face when two of the merchantmen collided. Several more collided as they tried to dodge the debris that spewed out. Some evaded other ships only to run into asteroids. Even the destroyers were now focusing more on avoiding collisions than on their attack.

We're through the ships; now to clear the asteroids.

Gallant found himself in the field's densest area as the ships in the convoy continued to scatter.

He heard Kelsey curse as he wrenched the Eagle past an asteroid.

Too close.

The Eagle twisted and leaped in response to his thoughts. Then Kelsey cried, "Incoming missiles!" Out of ammunition, the Eagle had no way to defend itself. They avoided direct hits, but both missiles detonated nearby, and Gallant felt the Eagle shudder and buck as the plasma wave hit. Kelsey cried out in pain, but he didn't dare take his eyes off the asteroids ahead.

"Kelsey? What happened?"

Out of the corner of his eye, he saw Kelsey activate the fire-suppression system.

"Fire aft, suppression in effect now," she said through gritted teeth. "The aft electrical panels took the worst of the plasma hit, and I caught some shrapnel."

Gallant risked a quick glance over his shoulder and almost lost control of the Eagle. Kelsey grunted as she struggled to pull a piece of jagged metal from her lower torso. Another sprouted grotesquely from her leg. Smoke billowed from the burning electrical panels and the reek of toxic fumes filled the compartment.

Another missile exploded behind them with a blinding flash of light.

Turning his gaze back to their escape route, Gallant said, "Don't move. I'll get back there as soon as I can."

Propelling the fighter upward in a tight spiral away from the attacking Titan ships, he concentrated on his escape path. A few ship-killer missiles still trailed behind them. With thrusters at maximum, the fighter's engines strained to accelerate even as he ducked and wove among the asteroids.

After several more minutes, he found what he had been looking for—a planetoid big enough to hide the Eagle. He swerved behind it, a plan taking shape in his mind

Ejecting the fighter's garbage, Gallant released some plasma and fired his lasers into the cloud, creating an explosion. Then he dropped the Eagle to the surface of the planetoid and sank down into a crevice deep enough to hide his fighter and avoid radar detection.

He let out a long, slow breath, hoping that his garbage looked enough like ship debris to fool the Titans. With any luck, they'd think he'd been hit by one of the last missile strikes.

He waited, heart pounding, as Titan scouts passed by without seeing them. After a while, the radar screen was empty. The Titans had moved off.

Finally, he turned his attention to Kelsey. He caught his breath at the sight of her injuries, her body bleeding and broken.

"Kelsey, stay awake. Look at me! You're going to be OK."

He carefully pulled the metal shards out of her flesh and applied a tourniquet to her right leg to control the bleeding until he got it well bandaged. Kelsey grimaced and stifled a cry. He looked at her eyes, checking for signs of shock, as he injected a pain reliever. As the medication took effect, her contorted expression relaxed, and he relaxed with her.

"Thank you, Henry," she said, her chest heaving.

Gallant cleaned the rest of her wounds and burns. He kept talking, demanding answers to random questions, to keep her mind alert and active.

Once she was resting comfortably in the bunk, he turned his attention to the next set of problems.

The suppression system had put the fire out, but the Eagle was in shambles. The burned electric panels still sparked, and so much equipment from storage lockers was strewn about the floor he had trouble moving around the compartment. Setting his jaw, he set to work repairing the ship's systems.

Worst of all, the plasma hit had damaged his communications system. He had no way to warn Mars Station about the Titans' secret base.

THE GREAT ESCAPE

22

The Eagle's shadow crept across the wall of its hiding place, advancing like a sundial while Gallant dozed fitfully. Reserve canisters fed fresh oxygen into the cramped compartment. The lithium hydroxide crystals absorbed the exhaled carbon dioxide. By turning off their life-support system, he was able to reduce the electronic emissions, but the scant environment left him nauseated.

His movements were slow and labored as if his arms were on strike. When he spoke, his voice sounded strange to his own ears. Even simple tasks required intense concentration.

Still, his mind was active, considering and rejecting escape options. All of them were thwarted by the destroyers that roamed just outside their hiding spot. Foreboding hung over him, weighing him down as much as his weariness and worry.

Kelsey was sedated, lying quietly on the sleeping bunk at the bottom of the compartment. He told himself he had dressed her wounds as best as he could, but he knew she needed to get real medical care as soon as possible.

Every time the radar pinged, it lost contact almost immediately. The signal disappearing into the background of space and asteroids. Gallant lost and rediscovered enemy ships many times. He wondered whether the contacts were just a few ships crisscrossing through the asteroid field, or an entire armada on its way to Mars. When he could muster the strength, he worked on the ship's communications equipment. He hoped to alert Mars Fleet to the dangers hiding in the asteroid field.

Maybe they'd send a rescue ship.

Listening to the hiss of oxygen from the last canister, he knew he had to come up with a workable escape plan. Until the oxygen ran out, they might be killed or captured, but escape was still possible. Now they were out of time and options. He had no choice but to start up the environmental system and move out.

He knew the odds were against them. Kelsey's blood pressure was falling. The ship had no reserve oxygen if the environmental system failed. And at the inner edge of the belt the asteroids thinned out, providing less cover.

He couldn't play hide-and-seek with the Titans forever. Gallant calculated a winding escape path through the asteroid cluster toward Mars. Nevertheless, he made what he hoped would be a stealthy dash.

They meandered down a narrow alley of large rocks, twisting and turning until they felt their closest pursuers had lost track of them.

Kelsey's injury prevented her from helping, but they moved ghostlike, hoping to evade their pursuers.

Gallant had a vague sense of his location and an even vaguer sense of the direction of the escape.

In a weak voice, Kelsey said, "There."

Pointing the way.

Seeing the enemy coming closer, Gallant suspected they were still in pursuit. The area still reeked of danger, but he didn't want to give in to fear. They ducked under a large asteroid and hid in the dark place while they scanned around them.

Were we seen?

Several ships passed close.

Gallant counted to ten as the contacts faded. He was determined not to give himself away by moving too soon.

The silence deepened, and he cautiously squeezed the Eagle out of the narrow hiding place and peeked out. He couldn't see any ships close by, but still, he hesitated. Gasping for breath, heart pounding—every little movement seemed to threaten him.

Then he saw a formless blur of movement and tried to maneuver away . . .

BAM!

The next thing he knew, he was on his back. From the fleeting glimpse he had, he recognized that the Eagle had suffered from a near-miss explosion.

Gallant now weaved through a cloud of meteorites, and his pursuer fell back.

His mind tried to pierce the darkness and thread an escape route.

He pushed his engines to their maximum and hoped for the best.

How much longer until we're discovered?

How much farther to leave them all behind?

He pressed forward.

Once clear of the asteroid belt and with the Titans a safe distance behind them, Gallant risked a message to Mars Fleet. He warned them of the hidden base and requesting assistance.

A response came back promptly—a relief ship was on the way.

He said, "Kelsey, can you hear me? We're almost there. Hold on a little longer."

Rescuing hands gathered them to safety. Gallant grabbed the alien equipment, along with the memory chips on which he had recorded information about the enemy's base.

When he saw Kelsey was safely on the way to a medical facility, he told the captain what he had learned about the Titans. The captain relayed this information to Mars as quickly as he could. Gallant gave a breakdown of the Titan force and their fortresses and support facilities.

A lieutenant from the destroyer handed Gallant a message from the admiral. It included orders to report for debriefing as soon as he reached Mars.

When they reached Mars, Kelsey was moved to an emergency room under the care of a team of doctors. After eight hours of waiting, he learned that the surgery was extensive, and she had a lot of recovering to do, but she was off the critical list. Gallant closed his eyes and breathed a sigh of deep relief.

HAUNTING
MEMORIES

23

The viewport on battlecruiser *Superb*, the flagship of the Mars Fleet, gave Gallant a splendid view of the magnificent red planet. He had a few coveted minutes alone to reflect on the coming ordeal. He found little solace in the planet's familiar appearance because of its stark contrast to his last vision of Jupiter.

He was aware of the many warships orbiting nearby, but they didn't draw his attention. Instead, he continued to stare straight ahead, lost in thought. Finally, though, he turned away from the viewport and paced the length of the conference room. He paid no attention to the luxurious furnishings and decorations. The oversized chamber was typically reserved for dignitaries visiting the fleet's flagship. Its walls showed in lavish detail great feats of historical figures. The overall effect was imposing, as intended, but Gallant didn't even glance at them.

Instead, his mind rehashed the events and choices that had led him to this room. Despite his disquiet, he congratulated himself on remaining calm. He expected a fierce grilling from the fleet's System Intelligence Agency (SIA). He smiled to himself. He forced his mind to function smoothly and efficiently. He even imagined he could hear meteorites pelting the *Superb* with a rat-a-tat sound just as they did against his Eagle. But of course, the armored hull made that impossible.

The pacing helped stretch his stiff back and legs. He had hated the enforced confinement of the Eagle.

While he waited, he fussed over his wounded arm, not because of the pain, but because the bandage bulged beyond the cuff of his jacket. Self-consciously he tugged at the sleeve, trying to hide the wrappings.

As the appointed hour approached, he took his seat at the ornate table with his back to the entrance, drumming his fingers on the polished top. The memory chips containing the video, data, and logs from the Eagle were in a pile to his right. On his left sat the Titan AI CPU unit. He looked away, not wanting to relive the fight in the saucer. Intent on organizing his thoughts, he didn't even notice when the viewport turned black.

He jumped at the voice behind him. "Do you mind if I sit here?"

He looked over his shoulder and saw a woman in her early twenties. She was dressed in a sharply pressed uniform with lieutenant stripes. Her blond hair was neatly trimmed above her shoulders. She looked fresh and rested as if just getting started rather than winding down after a long workday. She carried a large briefcase brimming with documents and an armful of computer paraphernalia. He couldn't help glancing around one more time.

Where is the fearsome interrogation team?

"Do you mind?" she repeated. "The senior officers will arrive soon, and the table will be full once everyone gets here, but I need to resolve some preliminary issues. Then we can proceed with the debriefing," she said, extending her hand. "I'm Julie McCall, SIA."

She flashed a radiant smile that both reassured and calmed Gallant.

"Henry Gallant," he said automatically, rising from his seat to shake her hand.

"Oh, yes, I know," she chuckled. "Would you like some coffee? It's the real stuff."

She swiped her comm pin over the room's automated dispenser and collected two cups.

"Cream and sugar?" she asked over her shoulder.

"Is that real too?" he marveled.

She nodded with a smile. "Yes, to both."

She tapped a couple of virtual buttons, and the dispenser delivered the steaming coffee.

"Thank you," he said, picking up the hot cup

cautiously, then curving his hands around its warmth to ward off the ship's dank, reprocessed air. He added, "You expect a crowd? I guess everyone's interested, but I already sent digital copies of my report, as detailed as I could make it. I don't know what else I can add."

"True, but with information this important, it's essential to get everything in the right context. Every nuance is vital," she said, setting up her computer.

She gave him another broad, disarming smile. "Besides, we may glean a few more details from you yet."

He studied her surreptitiously over the rim of his coffee cup.

She was tall and slender with a warm, inviting face. He surmised that she was good at getting people to reveal secrets, which made him want to come across as confident and imperturbable. Inwardly he lamented the newly requisitioned but as-yet-untailored service dress blue uniform.

She suggested, "Tell your story openly—hold nothing back. Sometimes talking to a total stranger is easier than to people you know. My staff won't be here for a while yet, so while we wait, let me validate this evidence and get your signature on your report and deposition. We can get into the narrative later."

His mind flashed to the events of the past days, but he shook the image off. He said, "The Jupiter battle, the asteroid belt, the escape—it's nearly a continuous blur now."

"Let's start with something concrete, like an

inventory of these chips," she said. The validation of the chips and his report went quickly. He signed his report and deposition without reading either.

She said a few unintelligible words into her comm badge and pulled a stack of papers from her briefcase. Starting with broad questions, she soon delved more deeply into the details of the trip. She asked about the number of Titan ships and their characteristics. After about twenty minutes, she looked toward one of the room's viewscreens with a nod. Gallant realized for the first time that their conversation was being monitored, even likely recorded.

He tensed at the sound of approaching footsteps.

As the door opened, he rose and stood at attention.

"At ease," one officer said, though Gallant wasn't sure who.

Raising his coffee mug for another sip, Gallant watched over the lip of the cup as they situated themselves around the table. He scanned each face in turn. None of them said anything to him as they took their places.

Gallant was conscious of his heart beating rapidly. Suddenly longing for the solitude of the Eagle, he wished he could get up and leave but knew that was impossible. He was at the mercy of the debriefing officers. As a senior captain took the seat next to him, he lowered his cup and set it on the table, trying not to spill the coffee.

The captain's smile was fleeting, his face serious. "I'm Captain Samuel Wilcox. I spoke with you earlier about the briefing, remember?"

Gallant only nodded. He was distracted by a trio of technicians who swarmed in. One set up a video feed, another copying the data chips to a tablet, and the third prepping a recording device.

Even after the seats at the table filled up, senior officers kept filing in. They lined up along the walls, waiting expectantly. Gallant blinked in surprise. The reports of his trip had spread more than he thought. Looking around the table, he saw Admiral Collingsworth, commander of the Mars Fleet, and swallowed hard.

It was clear that they had already been thoroughly briefed and had seen the Eagle's video and AI records. However, all this information was provided in bits and pieces. They wanted Gallant to put all the events in context from one image to the next. Also, Gallant's exceptional neural interface abilities gave him the best overall perspective of the battle. There was a myriad of details any intelligence officer would be dying to ask. Only Gallant could create a comprehensive tapestry of events.

As Lieutenant McCall nodded at him with an encouraging smile, Gallant stood up, glancing at the crowd again. Haltingly at first, then with increasing confidence, he relayed what he had learned about the Titan fleet in the asteroid belt. Questions pelted him, demanding, and badgering as if he were an enemy prisoner rather than a fellow officer. Gallant kept his composure and answered as best he could. Even so, he was painfully aware that his initial report now seemed inadequate.

Next, Captain Wilcox took over the questioning, probing into Gallant's background—his childhood, his family, his time on Mars, and his life at the academy. Gallant grew frustrated. He wanted to talk about the aliens, not himself. But Wilcox would not be deterred. He questioned methodically, learning about Gallant to gauge his credibility and reliability. When Wilcox seemed satisfied, he gestured to the man who sat directly across the table.

"Mr. Gallant, this is Captain George Ellison, intelligence officer for Mars Fleet. He has some questions for you."

Ellison seemed to be an imaginative, quick thinker whose questions ran into each other on their way out of his mouth. He was particularly interested in Gallant's neural-interface imaging of the Titan force.

"We in the intelligence division want as much detail as you can give us on the Titan ships' missile capabilities and the fortresses you saw. Such knowledge will give us a more complete profile of the enemy than what we're getting from Jupiter Fleet," he said, his eyes probing.

Gallant answered the officer's questions in terse, precise statements.

Finally, Ellison said, "OK, Mr. Gallant, I think it's time for a change in process. We would like you to give a narrative of everything that happened in the asteroid belt, just as it happened, as best as you can remember."

Gallant hesitated.

"Tell us about the action," prompted Wilcox.

"Well . . ." said Gallant, biting his lip.

One of the flag officers accompanying the admiral said impatiently, "Speak up, man!"

Gallant took a breath and began his report. Occasionally someone asked a leading question that led him on a tangent and unfolded more of the story. Gallant struggled to speak without arrogance, but his sudden outpouring of words surprised even him. He tried to present facts, not offer opinions. A few times, Lieutenant McCall played a video taken from his Eagle that enriched his narrative.

He tried to explain the effort, tension, and anguish that had overcome him as he struggled to navigate through the maze of asteroids. Then he detailed his actions and maneuvers as he fought the many Titan ships and evaded their missiles and plasma bursts. He described how he made the Titans believe that his ship had been destroyed. Finally, he spoke poignantly about how he had treated and cared for Kelsey as he repressed the concern that clutched at his throat.

At one point, he stopped, for the first time, feeling the pressure of all the historical figures on the walls looming over him. He blushed, suddenly afraid he'd been indiscreet or sounded boastful.

He looked around the table, expecting to see judgment or scorn. To his surprise and relief, he saw officers nodding in approval, maybe even admiration. The thought flashed through his mind that they might even envy his adventure. Every officer at the table was his senior, with vast experience in warships, men who had traveled from Earth to the outer reaches of the Jupiter frontier. Yet here they sat, captivated by his tale.

As he stammered to a conclusion, he felt disconcerted that he may have won their approval under false pretenses. He had never revealed his many fears during the horror of the battle. He hadn't included his haunted memories of his lost comrades on the Jupiter frontier or the many questionable choices he had made.

The officers began praising him for his single-handed attack on alien vessels and for retrieving the critical AI CPU. They were jubilant over his discovery of the hidden alien fleet. Gallant's fighter-pilot bravado had given them a spark of how to fight their opponent. They expressed lively pleasure at his safe return, but he could sense that they were still thirsty to know even more. When it was finally clear that they had completely exhausted him, they called a break. He used the time to rekindle his spirits.

When they resumed the session, Wilcox focused his intense gaze on Gallant and said, "It's clear that the United Planets have a dangerous adversary. Tell me about the Titan ship. Why did you pick this device out of everything in the aliens' control room?"

"I thought it resembled our AI processors."

"Did you compare it with the neural interface in your Eagle?"

"We did, briefly. It's very different from our interface, which allows me to draw information from the AI, but the system never controls my actions."

Gallant paused and looked around the table before continuing. "I believe the Titan interface both directs and coordinates the impulses of multiple individuals simultaneously. I suspect it also allows the AI to direct individuals' actions."

"What have you learned from the CPU and your experience with the Titan forces?" asked Wilcox.

Gallant said, "They have a distinctly different culture from us. It filters down into their command-and-control system, even their navigation tactics and attack formations. They don't act as independent individuals—not that they have a collective consciousness, or one mind telepathically controlling everything. I also don't believe they're cyborgs or controlled by artificial intelligence. My best guess is that they operate under limited AI capabilities and highly cooperative limited telepathy."

The next day, Gallant went to the Mars Station hospital to visit Kelsey. Instead of a sterile hospital room full of tubes and instruments, the room looked as if it might have been transplanted from her Oregon home. It was complete with holographs of personal items and photos of her family. Soothing music played quietly in the background. Unobtrusive monitors hidden under her bed kept the nursing station informed of her condition.

Gallant was relieved to find her sitting up in bed. She was still groggy from the medications and took a few minutes to recognize him, but when she did, she reached a hand toward him and said, "Henry! You're all right!"

"How are you?"

"Much better. They tell me it'll take time, but I should recover fully."

She hesitated at Gallant's silence. "Did you tell SIA about ..."

"Everything."

Finally, relieved of all his responsibilities, Gallant realized he too should see his doctor again. Underneath Kelsey's wrappings, his wounded arm was beginning to chafe and itch. In the urgent-care clinic, a nurse greeted him as he signed in and led him to a treatment room.

"Tsk, tsk. You should have come in for professional care," she said, shaking her head in disgust as she unwound the bandage. "This is a serious wound, although I must admit the first treatment looks quite competent."

Gallant suppressed a smile and said, "Sorry,

ma'am, but I was . . . delayed."

The nurse bustled about the room, prepping him for treatment with an antiseptic spray and draping a sterile cloth across his arm. Then she administered an analgesic and set out the tools for the doctor's treatment.

COMING HOME

24

Gallant started the next day feeling out of sorts and somewhat lost. He was like a weathervane swinging in the wind trying to find its bearing.

The significant events in the news weighed on his mind. Scout ships reported no hostile activity from the Titan force in the asteroids. The United Planets' Navy had opted to remain in orbit around Mars.

With events tense but uncertain, he was given a few days' liberty. However, since he had no family to visit, he was without a sense of direction.

The Mars weather remained temperate. The potent storms of winter had not yet arrived, leaving the sky clear. New Annapolis, the center of the Martian government and home to Mars Fleet Command, was an ultramodern city located near the planet's equator. It was bustling with business and tourist attractions. Its rustic colonial look was designed to reflect its namesake. Commercial buildings towered over smaller local establishments. The people lived and worked in much the same way that their ancestors did on Earth. Merchants and laborers scurried about the spaceport with cargo of every description. Flying cars used the low Martian gravity as they stacked up high above the city during the early-morning commuter traffic. The suburbs were packed with families thriving in this prototypical twenty-second-century colonial settlement.

Gallant remained at loose ends as he walked through town. He trudged along with a placid face and hoped to find something to pique his interest.

Recently built canals crisscrossed the entire planet. They channeled water from reservoirs and lakes to irrigate crops and supply cities. Small ferries navigated the smooth waters toward a junction where the canal flowed into the powerful New Severn River. Recent rains had swollen the river, and it swept past the wharves and shoreline buildings of Mars Fleet Command with a constant roar.

A little farther along the river, he reached the site of the Space Academy. Memories of his time there came flooding back. They reminded him of a time when he had fallen through the cracks of society and slipped down into an invisible world where "better" people ignored Naturals.

Now he noticed the academy graduates touring the area with their families.

One familiar face popped up in front of him.

It was his friend, Sam Wellman, who was currently serving as an astrogator on the *Superb*.

Sam greeted him, "Henry, it's great to see you." As tall as Gallant, but more solidly built, Sam was a rugged-looking young man.

Gallant's face lit up, and Sam's firm handshake put him at ease.

Sam said, "You'll have to fill me in on your adventures. There's a round of beer in it for you." Sam's eyes strayed to the heavy bandage Gallant still wore, and he asked, "How's your arm?"

"My arm's fine." Gallant had intended to spend the night at the academy's Bachelor Officer's Quarters (BOQ), but when he started to take his leave, Sam interrupted him. "No way! You're coming home with me. You know my parents. They'll want you to visit for a while."

"Thanks," said Gallant, smiling with delight. "That sounds good to me."

The pair made their way to a transit tube where they zipped along underground to the suburbs. When they emerged, they walked down the street leading to the Wellman family home.

"Henry," asked Sam, "do you remember these ladies?" As he spoke, an older woman motioned from the front door, and a young girl stuck her head out of the front window. Both women waved to the midshipmen. Sam's father came out to greet the young men.

Facing Gallant was a grungy, raggedy old man,

very much like a scarecrow with a scraggly white beard.

Gallant smiled. "Hello Mr. Wellman."

Mr. Wellman said, "Henry Gallant! It's good to see you again. Please, come in."

A few long strides brought Gallant to the entrance.

He said, "Mrs. Wellman, I'm so glad to see you again."

He squawked as she squeezed him in a bear hug. She had known Gallant since his plebe year and considered him to be one of her own offspring. She seemed obliged to gather the family around her. Her sense of motherhood made her something fierce and radiant, as if the world could not contain her.

Her daughter Kayla was just thirteen years old, but she already found midshipmen fascinating. She smiled up at Gallant. Three additional small children ran around.

Gallant entered the modest house, feeling heartened by the words of welcome. The walls were covered with pictures of the family, each child in several poses over several years. The carpets were synthetic fabric, durable but plain. The furniture was mass-produced prefabricated because the wood on Mars was a rare and expensive commodity. The environmental air controls were going full blast because so many doors and windows were open. Even though terraforming had brought Mars near to Earth's air-quality standards, the buildings still maintained environmental controls for indoor comfort. Despite all that, it was the most hospitable home Gallant had ever entered.

It was full of noise, clutter, and, most of all, young children. It smelled of promise. Boys and girls of every size and description scurried all over the place, playing and engaging in hijinks. Two large rooms on the right side had obviously been converted into playrooms. Several lads were playing an animated game on the floor while a tall youth practiced the violin in one corner. The room on the left had been converted into a makeshift dining room with a long table. The table was set with pitchers of milk, piles of bread, and platters of delicious-looking food. Gallant hesitated to move out from the shelter of the front hall. He remained standing, worried about being run down in a brisk game of tag he saw.

"No, they're not all ours," laughed Mrs. Wellman, patting his shoulder.

Mr. Wellman chuckled and said, "You picked a busy night for a visit. We're babysitting some of the neighbors' children while they're at a local event. Don't worry, they'll tire themselves out before long, and eventually, their parents will take them home."

"You'll stay the night, Henry?" asked Mrs. Wellman. Her gentle, soothing tone was as if she were addressing an awkward child.

Gallant found himself drawn like a compass arrow to be part of this family. It was one of those things he wanted so much that it was buried deep in the center of himself.

"Of course, he will," said Sam.

They looked expectantly at Gallant as if they'd been singing a song and paused for him to finish the reframe.

"Yes. Thank you so much."

"Wonderful. That's settled then. Let's get dinner underway. The little ones are ready for that," said Mrs. Wellman beaming. "Oh, by the way, John, you should look at Kayla's report card."

Gallant could tell that Mr. Wellman wasn't pleased with what he saw as he opened the card.

"Gee, Dad, you're soooo funny when your face gets all red!" exclaimed Kayla, brushing her red hair out of her twinkling green eyes.

John Wellman pursed his lips and rose to his full six-foot-two height. Then he broke into a broad grin and leaned over to kiss his daughter.

"Well, I wouldn't get so red if you spent as much time on your schoolwork as you do texting your girlfriends," he said.

Turning to his wife, he added, "She's still texting just girlfriends, isn't she? No boyfriends yet?"

"Mom!!" Kayla howled.

"She's growing up, John," said Mrs. Wellman, trying to suppress a laugh as she carried a stack of dinner plates to the table.

Soon the table conversation was interrupted as the children became more rambunctious. Gallant relished the chaos and warmth of the Wellman's home.

Hours later, as he lay in a bed in the quiet, dark spare room, Gallant listened to the many small sounds a house makes. He heard the ticking of the grandfather clock and the snoring of its inhabitants.

He slept better than he had in a long time.

RISK

25

he following day, Gallant received orders to brief government officials at Mars Fleet Command. He noticed a conspicuous calm among the population, even while the news of the Titan threat spread.

When he arrived at command headquarters, he presented his comm pin to the security officer. He was instructed to proceed to a large conference room on the fifth floor. The conference room turned out to be closer to the size of an auditorium.

Taken aback by the austere gathering of powerful people, he had the impression that the briefing was not going to be merely a formality.

The focal point of the room was a single chair next to a small table. Several larger tables and many rows of audience seats were in front. The first table was reserved for nine senators; their nameplates lined up in an imposing row. Senator Graham was the committee chairman presiding over a senatorial investigation. Behind each senator clustered several staffers. Behind them were two rows of civilians, including NNR president, Gerald Neumann. Behind this group were several rows of reporters and other media personalities. At the very back of the packed room was a line of military officers, including some that Gallant recognized from his debriefing two days before.

Admiral Collingsworth stood in the back of the room.

Gallant remained at attention, shifting his weight uneasily.

"Please take your seat and make yourself comfortable, Mr. Gallant," said the committee chairman, Senator Graham, smiling broadly for the television cameras strategically placed throughout the room.

What have I walked into?

Gallant sat down in the chair before him. On the table in front of him were the memory chips containing his data and ship's log along with his deposition.

"We're so glad you were available to give testimony before this committee," said Senator Graham. He turned toward the back of the room and nodded at Admiral Collingsworth.

"Let me describe how the Armed Services Oversight Committee will exercise its responsibilities."

Once more, he glanced over his shoulder

at Admiral Collingsworth, as if daring anyone to challenge him.

He continued, "This is an informal fact-finding inquiry into the recent military actions at Jupiter and in the asteroid belt. We will be evaluating the current conduct of the Titan war. This hearing will be recorded, and an unclassified edited version of these proceedings may be released to the public.

"To begin, I will read my formal opening statement for the record. Each senator will also provide a written copy of their statement to be included in the transcript."

As Chairman Graham read his statement out loud, the audience grew restless. His statement was nothing more than a bland summary of the military activity and related political events.

Graham banged his gavel several times to restore order. Then he said, "Let's review your activities and the data you collected, Mr. Gallant."

Step by step, Graham took Gallant through his report. The court members and the audience listened attentively to the summary account of each action.

"This report is a credit to you and Midshipman Mitchel," said the chairman. "You uncovered information vital to our safety."

"Thank you, Senator. We benefited from a great deal of good fortune," said Gallant.

"Really?" said the chairman, with a tinge of doubt in his voice. "Now let's get to the primary focus of this inquiry. That is the gross negligence of the armed forces to prevent the Titans from threatening first Jupiter and now Mars."

Graham's tone had a distinctive animus. A pained atmosphere descended over the room.

Gallant couldn't determine who this bombastic rhetoric favored, but he knew it could hardly be more ill-conceived. He felt it could lead to a whole series of strategic and psychological blunders by the government leadership.

Chairman Graham turned and said, "I yield the floor to Senator Chaffee for initial questioning."

Senator Chaffee sat on Graham's right. He was a dogged and fixated man, meticulous in his duties as he leafed through some of the papers in front of him. He too greeted the television cameras with a smile. "Mr. Gallant, during the Jupiter action, did you receive authorization to disengage from the battle at any time?"

"No, sir."

"Did you receive authorization to enter the alien destroyer and engage in hand-to-hand combat?"

"No, sir."

"Do you understand the difference between taking a risk and being reckless, Mr. Gallant?"

"I took a risk appropriate to the threat we faced, sir," said Gallant, uneasy with the line of questioning.

"Did Captain Caine give you advance classified orders to seek out a damaged Titan ship, in order to collect secret information and return it to him?" asked Chaffee, leaning forward in his chair and ignoring the hush that fell over the room.

"Huh? Uh, no, sir." Gallant thought the factual

record had been sufficient to evaluate his actions. So, he was surprised at the sharp questioning and accusations of errors in judgment.

The tension in the room mounted. A sense of mistrust had given birth to strident questions. With each inquiry, it became clear to Gallant that he was being investigated for possible dereliction of duty and overstepping his authority. He realized he could face a court-martial for conduct prejudicial to good order and discipline of the service. Against this array of potent charges by powerful individuals, he had only himself for defense.

"Did you get authorization for the abnormal flight path you took through the asteroid belt?"

"No, sir," answered Gallant, clenching his teeth.

"Had Captain Caine's radar scans already revealed the location of the Titan base in the asteroids? Did he send you there deliberately? Did he withhold this information from higher authorities?"

"No, of course not!"

Gallant's cheeks were flushed, and his neck had turned bright red. He was out of his depth, and he knew it. He felt he was being attacked unfairly, but he was helpless to protest. Slowly, it dawned on him that he might not be the target of the attack. They might be going after Captain Caine.

Gallant looked suspiciously at the NNR president, Gerald Neumann, who sat directly behind the senators.

"How did Jupiter Fleet let the enemy slip past them to establish a secret base in the asteroid belt?

Tell us, how was that possible?"

Gallant tried to choose his words carefully. "I don't know, sir, but the solar system is quite large, and they could easily have moved in while Jupiter was at a different point in its orbit. Asteroid and planet shadows also often obstruct radar scans. I took advantage of that myself when I was hiding from the Titans."

Chaffee shifted in his seat, leaning over to hear a message one of his staffers passed from Gerald Neumann. Then he said, "Why was Captain Caine reluctant to provide escorts for convoys?"

Gallant recalled that Caine had discussed this in front of him, but he was reluctant to reveal too much, "Uh . . . Captain Caine made every effort to supply convoy escorts while providing for the defense for Jupiter Station."

"Do you have any reason to doubt Captain Caine's loyalty? To your knowledge, has he withheld vital information from the proper authorities?"

"No," responded Gallant, tight-lipped, pointedly omitting the *sir*. Then he added, white-hot with anger, "Captain Caine is a brilliant and courageous officer. I have the greatest respect for him, and for all the officers in Jupiter Fleet. They have placed their lives in jeopardy."

Senator Chaffee sat quiet for a minute as if debating a change in tactics. Then he asked, "Why did you delay transmitting a warning to Mars Fleet that a Titan armada was hiding in the asteroid belt? Wasn't it your sworn duty to raise the alarm?"

"I calculated the strategic advantage to be gained if I could get away stealthily and report to Admiral Collingsworth."

"The standing orders say to report enemy activity immediately. Who gave you the authority to make strategic decisions beyond your rank? Do you regret your actions?"

Gallant said, as forcefully as he could, "If I had a chance to do it over, I would take the same actions."

I'm a pawn in a larger game against the military.

When Chaffee was finished, he yielded to other senators. They continued to lambast Gallant. He responded in monosyllables, numbed by the hypocrisy.

After the hearing, Gallant was surprised to be asked to visit Gerald Neumann in his suite at the New Annapolis Hilton Hotel. A limousine was waiting for him. The last thing Gallant wanted to do was face another inquisition, but he couldn't think of a way to decline gracefully.

Maybe he just wants to ask about his son.

A doorman dressed in a flashy uniform with many buttons and flourishes greeted Gallant. He handed him off to a tuxedoed butler, who escorted him to the hotel's premier suite. As he entered, his mouth dropped open. The suite was luxurious beyond anything he had ever imagined. Paintings by old masters hung on the walls; oriental carpets of ancient weave padded the expensive-looking tile. Furniture from Earth's history long past adorned the rooms. The windows offered stunning views of the Mars landscape. The opulence was so excessive that Gallant was embarrassed to think that such extravagance existed in a universe where ordinary people barely scraped out a meager existence.

Another butler led Gallant inside and showed him to a chair, offering him dessert and refreshments. Gallant sat in uncomfortable silence for half an hour before Neumann arrived.

Gerald Neumann was tall and fit, strikingly handsome and young for his fifty-five years. He walked up to Gallant with his hand extended.

"Let me say how impressed I am with your heroic journey and your obviously exceptional talents."

Gallant said, "Thank you, sir."

"I hope this visit isn't inconvenient. My son has spoken of you several times. He is doing fine, by the way. I just received an update on his recovery."

Gallant said, "I'm glad to hear that, sir. He's an outstanding pilot and respected by all aboard *Repulse*."

"That's fine. Now, I'd like to tell you a little about myself," said Neumann with a smile that looked unpleasantly like the forced joviality on the faces of the senators.

"Sir?"

"I was born on April 17, 2115, in New York City. After working for my father, who was a highly successful shipping and mining businessman,

I started my own company in 2138. In my early years, I learned much from my father that proved vital to my later success. My father was a leading industrialist who taught me the essentials of good business. I learned about management and how to reorganize enterprises into conventional joint stock corporations. I envisioned an integrated industry that would cut costs, lower prices to consumers, and produce in greater quantities. These skills were the foundation of my first investments. When I consolidated the mining business, the newspapers made accusations about my tactics. But I have always maintained excellent relations with politicians who helped me resolve public issues. The company I built was the first major business on Mars, and today NNR remains the largest. I have always been sharp in realizing any advantage I can find. I often sought out distinct technologies that gave me leverage over my competition."

Neumann clearly enjoyed talking about himself. He snapped his fingers, and a butler appeared with a cigar. The butler offered a light, and Neumann puffed on the cigar before continuing. "During my career, I've accrued wealth, power, and influence, but I've also attracted a lot of media scrutiny. Now many of the UP industries are in the hands of a few powerful business leaders, including myself. I have been criticized for creating monopolies and making it difficult for other businesses to compete against me. Needless to say, such accusations never bother me." Neumann patted himself on the chest as he spoke.

"Sometimes, one individual can impose order and structure on an otherwise chaotic situation. Such a person rises above the common man."

He took another puff on his cigar. "My first marriage to Amelia Theodore was brief. She died a few months after our Anton was born. Five years later, I remarried." He cleared his throat and continued, "I have many interests beyond the world of shipping, however. I enjoy sailing and won the Earth's Cup yacht races several times. As you can see, I am an ardent art collector and have an extensive collection." He waved his hand at some of the examples before them.

"Today, I dominate two industries—space shipping and mining. I am also interested in anti-proton fuel production, a crucial material in our future growth within the solar system. You can see, my interests are extensive."

Gallant remained silent. Neumann said, "My son sent me some information about you. That, plus everything I've learned from the hearing about your unique abilities, leads me to an inescapable conclusion. You have significant potential, and so you interest me."

He continued, "I've explained all this to you because I want you to understand what an extraordinary opportunity it is to work for me. You will be invaluable to me in directing commercial shipping safely and efficiently on optimal routes. I will make it well worth your while, and you needn't concern yourself any further with court-martial charges or investigations. It's a simple matter to have you reassigned to me, or even released from military service altogether if you prefer.

He waited for a long moment, and then added, "In every crisis, there is risk and opportunity. Leave the fighting to others. Why should you take the risk? Take the opportunity instead."

Gallant couldn't restrain himself. "We have very different opinions about what is valuable in life. There is nothing you can offer to make me shirk my duty or my shipmates."

EVALUATION

26

Gallant stood at attention in Admiral Collingsworth's office in New Annapolis. The room was slightly old fashioned, even Old World. Gallant would not have been surprised to see it at the Naval College on Earth. In fact, it was a near-replica of the office of the Commandant of the Space Academy, which Gallant had once visited. Nonetheless, it was equipped with the latest technology required for conducting military assessments.

The admiral also appeared Old World. Though he was rather short and wizened, his uniform was immaculately tailored. He glanced at Gallant, sizing him up, comparing the report on the paper on his desk with the midshipman standing before him. He frowned repeatedly and asked questions of his chief of staff, murmuring so Gallant couldn't hear.

The admiral's chief of staff, Captain William

Pierce, hovered around the admiral, whispering last-minute information. He presented virtual screen readouts and updates on fleet activities and a comparison of strength against the Titans. SIA input adjustments based upon Gallant's debriefing were shown in red on the screen. After several minutes, he nodded toward Gallant and spoke rapidly in the admiral's ear. The admiral stood up and began pacing.

"When I was asked to make you available for a briefing to the Senate's Armed Services Oversight Committee, I was not informed of its nature," said the commander-in-chief of the Mars Fleet. His voice was harsh and strained. He paused and then added, almost under his breath, "It's unfortunate, but the field of battle isn't the only place you'll face enemies."

Although the admiral didn't openly express his opinion of the committee's behavior, Gallant judged that he was seething to say more.

Collingsworth walked to the far wall and looked out the window. After a minute, he had visibly regained his equanimity. "You may rest assured, however, there will be no further action taken against you. Your record will reflect your honorable service and valor."

"Thank you, sir," said Gallant.

Collingsworth returned to his ornate chair and sat down. "You may have wondered why the SIA spent so much time questioning you about your personal background, at home, at the academy and on *Repulse*. I ordered that. I've found over the years that written words are sterile, not enough to take the measure of a man. Your recent accomplishments are unique, and I needed the most complete picture of you possible to form an unbiased opinion."

He smiled slightly. "I like officers who are bright and inventive and willing to fight despite the odds."

Let me tell you about some changes I'm making. I'm converting some fighters to carry anti-ship missiles, creating a new kind of bomber. The bombers are expected to carry just four anti-ship missiles, but they will give up their antimissile missiles to make room. That's why they'll need fighter escorts."

Gallant said, "Bombers could change the dynamics of battle. They'll give our small craft some real firepower, sir."

"The new weapons should be effective in fighting the Titan forces. The new ships could be forerunners of a weapon capable of affecting the balance of power. Still, fighter pilots are fighter pilots, and converting their ships to act as bombers might be resisted," said Collingsworth.

Gallant's experience convinced him that the Eagle fighters were too small to take on the Titan destroyers by themselves. But in combination with the new bombers, they could be a deadly weapon.

The Admiral said, "I've been delaying the fleet's departure because I'm waiting for these bombers."

He leaned forward and looked carefully at Gallant before continuing, "You've had quite an adventure. I'm not exactly sure what to make of it, but I'm particularly impressed with your neural interface abilities. Your unique ability to visualize and understand so much of the battlefield may be significant."

He paused again and then said, "I have plans for you."

Outside the admiral's office, Gallant found Lieutenant McCall waiting for him.

"Please follow me," she said and led him to the second floor of the building and into the Mars Fleet Command's CIC.

McCall said, "The news you brought has had an electric effect on the fleet and changed the outlook of the people as well. We've been more than a little overwhelmed in the intelligence community. Things can't stay static much longer. Nevertheless, Admiral Collingsworth is still debating the best course of action for the fleet."

Gallant frowned.

"We just received a data dump from a drone monitoring Ceres," said McCall. "I'd like you to compare its information against the data you collected. In addition, your mental image of the Titan base could prove helpful."

Gallant nodded as he took a seat at a computer station to begin comparing his collected data against the new information. The Titan disposition didn't appear to have changed significantly since his encounter.

He said, "I imagine the Titan leadership is wondering why Mars Fleet is taking so long to come to the aid of Jupiter."

"Admiral Collingsworth has received reinforcements from Earth. He's calculated the minimum strength required to safeguard Mars and how many ships he can safely take into battle," McCall said. "First, he'll establish a line of communication to support his fleet's movements, then move deep into the asteroid field before he turns toward Ceres. He wants to catch the Titans by surprise."

She added, "He wants you to verify the battlecruisers, fortresses, and supply stations within the asteroid cluster. How sure are you of the plots and details that you provided about their methane production?"

"Midshipman Mitchel and I were careful to get the deposition and numbers of enemy ships. We noted the positions of fortresses and support facilities."

McCall said, "That's still not a guarantee that you saw the entire base. The tempo of war is quickening. We are preparing fleet movements to transport fuel and supplies. No detail is too minor for evaluation. Thanks to you, we may be able to exploit the vulnerability in the Titan deployment. The biological cells you collected from the crippled Titan destroyer are invaluable. We are learning about how a methane-based life-form survives. You gave us a treasure trove."

After a while, she was satisfied, so they moved on to consider the AI CPU device that Gallant had recovered from the Titan destroyer.

McCall explained, "The human brain is composed of billions of tiny, interconnected neurons. The average human can think up to eighty thousand thoughts a day. Each thought creates a minuscule electrical discharge that can be measured by EEG. Every math calculation or word thought forms a unique wave pattern. The brain state produced by each thought results in different patterns of neural interaction. These patterns of waves are characterized by different amplitudes and frequencies. Neurons are constantly creating new connections between each other and severing old ones. When humans learn to associate things, the neurons fire together in a pattern, producing a brainwave that, with the help of a neural interface, can control a device. This makes it easier to reproduce the mental state at will."

Gallant listened attentively to McCall's description.

"You already know that your neural interface allows the AI to read your thought patterns and make your fighter respond. Each order you give to the Eagle's controls is a unique wave pattern. The neural interface interprets it to control the ship's systems."

Gallant said, "Midshipman Mitchel thought the Titan device showed telepathic capabilities."

McCall said, "She was right. Preliminary analysis of the alien AI CPU that you captured indicates that the aliens have a rudimentary form of telepathy. It combines telepathic communication and collective pattern recognition. It allows many individual Titans to create a single combined wave pattern for the AI to interpret. Their limited telepathy means that they can act individually, their thought processes can be collective. The resulting behavior is markedly different from humans. Their approach to problems and strategies will likely be very different."

Gallant asked, "Could this also explain why they have no small fighter craft?"

"What do you mean?"

"They may need several minds working in unison to form useful patterns for the neural interface and AI to interpret."

"I hadn't thought of that, but it makes sense," concluded McCall. She asked, "Would you mind if I ask something for my own curiosity?"

"Not at all."

"What does it feel like? I mean, when you're mentally visualizing all the ships and planets and everything, right in the middle of a battle?"

"The best illustration I can think of is that it's like being a quarterback on the football field. You think about what the opposing team may do and call a play. Once the ball is hiked, you sense where the pressure is to avoid being sacked. As the receivers run down the field, you analyze the defenders' coverage and finally throw the ball to the open receiver. If you've had a clear mental image of the defense and your own players, you should hit the receiver in stride, and he runs for a touchdown."

"You men and your sports analogies," snickered McCall.

"So, what are the fleet's plans for me?" Gallant asked, a little anxious about his future. "Am I going back to Repulse and Jupiter Station?"

She said, "Before Admiral Collingsworth decides on your role in future actions, he has ordered our med techs test your ability."

She led Gallant to her desk and pressed a call button. When an SAI officer appeared, she said, "This is Lieutenant Rudman. He'll do your evaluation on the interface."

As Rudman set up his apparatus, he explained how the evaluation simulator would test Gallant's response to various stimuli.

Wearing the AI simulator, Gallant saw a vast area of space. Natural obstacles and a variety of ships. After several intense hours of ship maneuvers, Gallant's brain felt like a wrung-out dishrag.

Then he had to wait another long half an hour while Rudman and McCall analyzed the results. He heard their whispers but was too exhausted to care what they'd learned about him.

Gallant waited, nursing a cup of real coffee while McCall reported their findings to Admiral Collingsworth. When she finally returned, she licked her lips and took a deep breath, clearly flustered. "Even though you're the product of natural selection, you were born with the enhanced enzymes necessary for a fighter pilot. Before you, only genetically engineered humans had these enzymes to operate the neural interface."

Gallant looked directly into McCall's eyes, trying

to read her emotions. She continued, "The admiral was looking for a more complete picture of your abilities and limitations. These tests, combined with the AI log from your Eagle, provide a comprehensive assessment of your current capabilities."

Gallant's curiosity increased at her discomfort.

McCall put her hands on the desk, trying to still their trembling, and said, "Your range of vision over the battlefield is unprecedented. You have a greater capacity for visualizing and evaluating individual objects than any other subject. The tests indicate that you are vastly superior to our strong-AI avatars, as well as the best of our genetically engineered pilots. Not only that, you may surpass even the collective pattern recognition of the Titans. In short, you may be one or more orders of magnitude superior to any other fighter pilot. Ever."

Gallant was stunned by the scale of her assessment.

"The admiral is assigning you to his staff aboard *Superb*. He intends to commit you to special missions as he sees fit. A new Eagle fighter is ready for you, and an astrogator will be assigned when you report to *Superb*'s Squadron 801."

"Would it be possible for Midshipman Sam Wellman to be my astrogator? I know him, and we make a good team," said Gallant.

"That should be no problem."

Gallant sat on the edge of Kelsey's hospital bed, trying not to smile as she erupted in laughter.

"It wasn't funny!" Gallant insisted. "Those senators roasted me from stem to stern."

"Oh Henry, keep your perspective. You went through worse hazing at the academy. Why can't you see the humor in it?" asked Kelsey, clearly enjoying his account of the hearing.

"Am I really that uptight?" he asked. "Suppose you explain the humor to me. Please, I'd like to understand."

"You did your duty. You did nothing wrong. The senators have no legitimate case against you." She sighed and placed her hand on his. "To politicians, perception trumps reality. They're all about creating a favorable public perception and aren't concerned about what's real or valid. In the end, all they've done is make themselves look ridiculous by condemning you for the vagaries of war. When you chase the Titans off the Jupiter frontier, they'll sing your praise louder than anyone and pretend they never doubted you."

"Kelsey, do you always see the rainbows—never the rain?" Gallant asked, joining in her laughter at last.

"Nonsense," she replied. "Don't you know that to a farmer, rain is better than rainbows?"

"I can't win against you," said Gallant. "Anyway, my meeting with the SIA officer, Lieutenant McCall, went well. She confirmed your analysis that the Titans are telepathic."

Kelsey nodded thoughtfully.

He hesitated a moment. "She also told me I'm being assigned to Squadron 801 on *Superb*. Sam Wellman will be my astrogator."

His voice trailed off on the last word.

"That's great. Sam is a good man," she said. "I wish I could go with you, but the doctors say I need physical therapy, along with at least one more surgery."

He was going to tell her more about the neural interface exam results, but this didn't seem the occasion to open that topic. No longer comfortable talking about important things, they drifted into more mundane topics. Soon, it was time for Gallant to leave.

"'Bye, Kelsey," he said, trying to dispel a vague sense of loss. He leaned over and gave her an awkward kiss on the cheek, acutely conscious of her nearness and the touch of her hand.

"Godspeed," she said, suddenly serious, knowing she wouldn't be with him for his next battle. She forced a smile and added, "See you on Jupiter Station."

ROCKS

27

Admiral Collingsworth led twenty-four battlecruisers, sixty cruisers, and over two hundred destroyers into the asteroid belt. The battlecruisers formed a three-dimensional diamond, an arrowhead with *Superb* at the tip. The cruisers constructed a sphere around them, with the destroyers making up a larger shell around the entire formation. The sunlight reflecting off the titanium hulls made the fleet look like a sparkling ball suspended in space.

The admiral relaxed in his command chair on the flag bridge. The main viewer showed a shower of tiny asteroids that pelted *Superb*'s shielded hull. As the ship moved through space, larger asteroids flashed by. Chief of Staff Captain William Pierce sat next to him to provide constant updates on ships, personnel, and orders.

Gallant sat in the ready room with the other

officers of *Superb*'s Squadron 801, awaiting orders to scramble. Comfortable in their form-fitting pressure suits, the pilots monitored the fleet's progress on the viewer screen. They were eager to meet the enemy, expecting a slugging match, and morale was high.

Rumors about Gallant's exploits had circulated widely, and the pilots peppered him with questions. He answered them, as he had all others, with short, specific facts and no bragging.

Thoughtfully, Sam pulled Gallant aside. Looking at Gallant's arm, he asked, "Henry, are you really ready?

"Don't worry, I'm fine. You've trained with me for the past week. Do you doubt I'm fit and ready to go?" said Gallant, leaning against the hatch that led to the fighter hangar bay.

"No, of course not," said Sam. He fidgeted a bit and then added, "I just wish they would make up their minds and let us launch already."

"We're still too far away to engage," said Gallant.

"Regardless, I wish we were going into action instead of spending so much time maneuvering about, while they think about it," said Sam.

"What a firebrand!" said Gallant, laughing.

"Me? No. I just mean . . . oh, I don't know what I mean," Sam said.

"Be patient," said Gallant, giving his friend a strained smile. "Our time will come soon enough." He looked at the viewing screen again and listened to the commands being transmitted to other ships. By switching communications channels, he could also eavesdrop on individual unit commands.

As the fleet approached Ceres, Admiral Collingsworth ordered a course change toward the planetoid. If the Titans were monitoring their progress, this move left no room for doubt about their intentions. By now, the Titans knew their secret base had been discovered, and any hope of getting behind the Mars Fleet and attacking Mars was over.

Orbiting Ceres was the Titan armada. It had twelve battlecruisers, seventy cruisers, and two hundred eighty-eight destroyers. The Ceres asteroid cluster was a complex mesh of asteroids orbiting in a static pattern. It created numerous voids and passages. There was only limited visual and radar detection possible due to the unusually high density. The Titans had built in-depth defenses. There were minefields and fortresses with overlapping fields of fire from scores of missile launchers.

The total number of missile launchers gave Admiral Collingsworth an advantage over the enemy. However, that was tempered by the presence of the fortresses. The question was whether the Titans would fight from behind their forts.

As the fleet approached Ceres, Admiral Collingsworth deployed the Mars Fleet. He divided it into three divisions. The first was led by Superb, with the main battle force. It had eighteen battlecruisers with a strong cruiser-destroyer escort.

The Second Division, commanded by Admiral Hue, was a close-in bombardment force. It had six battlecruisers with a cruiser-destroyer escort.

Admiral Collins commanded the Third Division, an assault force tasked with landing the Marines.

Gallant knew that Mars Fleet was powerful and well-prepared for action. Collingsworth hoped for a ship-to-ship engagement. The admiral's concern, however, was that the Titans might flee. On the other hand, if the Titan fleet did retreat, the fortresses would fall quickly under the onslaught of the Mars Fleet.

Gallant listened to the clamor coming from the hangar bay as the squadron's fighters completed their preflight checks. His adrenaline surged as he heard Admiral Collingsworth order the fleet to increase acceleration and close on Ceres.

The Titan armada was already evacuating facilities. Their warships headed toward deep space in a ragged formation, leaving the slower transport ships behind.

Sam said, "Look at the scope! They don't want to tangle with us. They're packing up and clearing out!"

Gallant said, "They're cutting their losses and abandoning the base. It looks like they're retreating toward Saturn, leaving their fortresses to fight a rear-guard action. I suppose they'll destroy as much of the facilities as they can."

Sam said, "You mean they'll destroy as much as Admiral Collingsworth gives them time for."

As the Titan armada moved out, Admiral Collingsworth ordered, "All ships, man battle stations." Gallant knew he had hoped for a decisive engagement but would have to content himself with destroying the base on Ceres.

Admiral Collingsworth led the First Division after the Titan armada to engage any Titan ships that might try to reverse course.

Second Division moved in to destroy the enemy fortresses. The Marine assault force was ready to root out the Titans entrenched in the facilities as soon as Second Division did as much damage as it could. Stretched within the asteroid defensive position were refueling stations. These were an important prize for the United Planets' fleet to capture.

"Inform me when Second Division reaches missile flight time of one hundred twenty seconds," Admiral Collingsworth said to *Superb's* commanding officer.

While *Superb* and the rest of First Division maintained their position between the enemy fleet and Ceres, Second Division closed on Ceres. An officer reported, "Missile flight time for Second Division is one hundred twenty seconds, sir."

"Very well," said Admiral Collingsworth. "Admiral Hue commence firing."

Second Division's battlecruisers began bombarding the powerful forts. They concentrated fire on the outer fortresses first. Admiral Hue dispatched a task force of cruisers and destroyers to target the space stations. Missiles battered the stations from both sides while the battlecruisers pounded the fortresses. A fleet of fighters put up a defensive screen of antimissiles to cover them.

The fortresses launched a heavy volley of fire at Admiral Hue's ships. Hue's ships spat out a flurry of missiles in response while their fighters kept up stout defensive fire. When the fortresses' fire dwindled, Admiral Hue ordered his ships to close on the targets, keeping up their barrage. Slowly, the fortresses were reduced, but not before taking out several destroyers and a couple of cruisers.

Although the interlocking missile batteries made an intimidating barrier, after a couple of well-aimed missiles, the forts were reduced to scattered rubble, belching smoke, and debris.

Admiral Hue's attack had crippled the enemy. He ordered, "Hard to port, come to course 120, azimuth up 10 degrees, at time 1626."

Admiral Collingsworth's voice crackled over the fleet-wide communications. "Third Division seize remaining fortresses and subdue any resistance. *Superb*, launch all fighters. Clear a path through those minefields."

"Launch all fighters! Launch all fighters!" blared the speakers in Squadron 801's ready-room. Pilots and astrogators scrambled into the hangar bay and began climbing into their Eagles.

Gallant heard Sam mutter, "About time," as they sealed the hatch.

He fidgeted in his seat, impatient for their turn on the launch catapult. The thrust of acceleration sent a familiar rush of adrenaline through him, and he shouted, "Let's go!"

Before he reached the minefields, Gallant was already picking out individual mines to blast.

"Satisfied?" asked Gallant.

"You bet!"

The fighters flew in a close formation, blasting everything in their path to secure a path through the mines. Forts on either side of the asteroid channel spit missiles at the fighters. The narrow channel was still treacherous.

Too bad Admiral Collingsworth didn't send some bombers with us.

He radioed to *Superb*, "The asteroid channel spirals to port with mines locked in orbit. It makes for some vicious crossfire. I recommend antimissile support."

The Squadron 801 commander responded, "Flights 1, 2, and 3, shift to missile defense."

Even with antimissiles, Squadron 801 took casualties. Gallant drove his Eagle in a twisting loop; the motion slamming him hard. Sam grimaced as an equipment locker burst open from the shock of a near miss. Some objects flew around the cabin as Gallant corkscrewed through the channel. A small fire started but Sam was quick with the fire suppressant.

"Thanks," a voice said over the local channel from a nearby shuttle. Gallant appreciated the simple acknowledgment and looked over his shoulder at Sam, who also looked pleased. The squadron could return to *Superb*.

As the Marines began landing, several explosions rocked the fortress—triggers designed to keep the facilities out of UP hands. The Marines barely hesitated before swarming through the remaining buildings. The Titans refused to surrender, opting to die in battle instead.

Soon the entire Ceres asteroid cluster and all its defenses were either wreckage or captured.

Admiral Collingsworth led the First Division in a brief chase after the Titan fleet, but they refused to engage. While the aliens streamed away, Collingsworth returned to Ceres to oversee the final clean-up of the Ceres base.

The Titan armada continued toward the outer planets until the next day when the fleet split in two. The larger force, which included all the slower battlecruisers, headed directly for Saturn. A smaller force of cruisers and destroyers headed for Jupiter at maximum acceleration. This second cruiser force was intended to reinforce the existing Titan cruisers at Jupiter. Given their head start of the Titan cruisers, Mars Fleet would not arrive in time.

Instead, Admiral Collingsworth sent six fighter squadrons and six bomber squadrons after the Titan fleet. They had the acceleration thrust to overtake the enemy. From the *Superb's* ready-room, the pilots again scrambled to their ships. There was a great deal of curiosity about their new mission.

Admiral Collingsworth opened a communications channel to address the flotilla crews. "Midshipman Gallant of Squadron 801 will command the flotilla. His exceptional ability with the neural interface will allow him to evaluate battle conditions and direct the attack. Captain Caine is expecting your reinforcements." He paused and then added, "Make your best possible acceleration to Jupiter. The flotilla's task is to engage and defeat all Titan forces threatening the frontier."

"Aye aye, sir," responded Gallant, his face determined.

Lieutenant McCall sent out a fleet-wide communication update. It stated that the Titans were fighting to the death. They would vent their methane breathing apparatus and commit suicide rather than be captured. In addition, they were setting explosives where possible. However, SAI had managed to gather some data files and information about the history of the Titans. SAI was able to interpret some of it. They learned that the Titans first came to the solar system about two centuries earlier. They initially settled on Saturn's moon Titan and began exploring the system for methane friendly locations. They eventually visited Earth and all the planets of the system but didn't communicate with humankind. SAI confirmed that the aliens originally came on a generation ship from the M3-type red dwarf Gliese 581. They began Gliese-forming the most methane-compatible moons of the outer planets. They built homes, industries, and facilities to provide for their civilization. When they came, their science was more advanced, but it took them a century to develop enough population and infrastructure. They built most of the Ceres base decades ago but only sent their armada there recently by stealthy means.

The Titans could communicate telepathically with each other, but not with humans. Having no vocal cords or speech boxes, they never developed a verbal means of communication. They tried and failed to understand human speech, though they had developed an understanding of human writing.

REDEMPTION

28

T he Titan cruisers and destroyers of the asteroids reinforced the original Titan force. They descended on Jupiter Station, bent on destruction. On Ganymede, the Titan ground forces burst from their bunkers, swarming Kendra. High above them, the Titan cruisers and destroyers from the first battle resumed their attack on Jupiter Station.

The remnants of the Jupiter Fleet, *Repulse*, *Renown*, and *Remarkable,* did what they could to repel the latest Titan offensive. The lone remaining destroyer *Madison* stood by.

Close behind the Titan fleet came the fighter and bomber from the Mars Fleet. The high-speed chase across space ended as the Titan focused their attack directly on the remaining UP battlecruisers.

Both outnumbered and outmatched by the numerous Titans, the UP fleet faced daunting odds. *Repulse* and *Renown* were reporting numerous missile hits and severe damage. *Remarkable* shuddered from numerous weapons blasts. And *Madison* disappeared in a tremendous explosion.

As his flotilla prepared to engage, the *Repulse* order the battlecruisers to move closer to Ganymede. They wanted to add firepower to the research lab's FASER cannon. A missile spat from *Repulse* and disintegrated an alien destroyer. The Titan forces concentrated their fire on *Remarkable*. Then the battle degenerated into a ship-to-ship free-for-all at close range. The space around Jupiter Station was cluttered with escape pods.

Over the general command channel, Captain Caine ordered, "All ships close on the enemy."

As the flotilla closed on its targets, Gallant scanned the battlefield through his neural interface. He let the position of all the ships unfold in his mind. He concentrated his inner vision and grasped the full scope of the battle situation. In a flash of insight, he saw a solution—a risky move that, if successful, would turn the tide of the battle in their favor. He sucked in a breath, hoping he could effectively coordinate two wings of the flotilla.

"Red Wing, attack from the sunward side of the Titans. Bombers release your first barrage of missiles at extreme range. Blue Wing, guide on me to attack from the opposite side."

Time seemed to slow as Gallant snapped out orders for assigned targets. He concentrated on the fighters needed to defend each bomber.

"Fire missiles!"

The Titan cruisers responded with decoys and electronic jamming. But the enhanced-UP missiles devastated cruiser after cruiser.

In the confusion, Gallant was surprised to identify two patched-up fighters launched from *Repulse*. He didn't realize that any had survived the last battle, but he used the neural interface to calculate their trajectory. On a secondary communications channel, he heard, "Save some for us, Henry."

"Yeah, Gallant. Squadron 111 has a score to settle."

Gallant grinned. "Red! Neumann! Great to have you guys here. Form with this half of Squadron 801." Gallant led his wing toward the Titans' flank.

Recovering from their confusion, the Titans launched a heavy missile barrage of their own. This time they aimed at the attacking flotilla rather than Jupiter Fleet.

This was the first time Gallant had been in a command position in battle. He was responsible for the actions and lives of so many others. The complex demands of keeping the flotilla coordinated were taxing.

Explosions across the battlefield distorted his image of the many ships. It made it hard for him to distinguish individual objects. He struggled to maintain his focus, but a series of missiles bracketed Gallant's Eagle, and he found himself in a desperate fight to stay alive. He drove the Eagle to avoid further shock waves and thermal blasts. He revved his engines. He drove the Eagle through a rapid series of twists, rolls, and banks that compressed him into his seat. The Eagle screamed in protest at the erratic acceleration maneuvers, and he wondered whether it would take the strain. Small internal fires sprang up in the cockpit, and Sam worked to contain them.

Blasting through a debris field, Gallant found a calmer section of space, and he began to take stock of the flotilla's condition.

But before he could get his bearings, a warhead exploded just to port. His Eagle threw out sparks and smoke belching from his console.

A second explosion sent a shock through Gallant's body. His head snapped back against the seat, then he slumped forward, unconscious.

Gallant's mind swam with nightmarish images —faces of his parents distorted with terror, the explosion of Sandy Barrington's Eagle, Kelsey's bleeding body. He heard her voice, pleading: "Henry, Henry!"

A slap on his face brought him back to reality. He blinked, trying to focus as the hand hit him again. Dimly he recognized the voice: Sam, not Kelsey, was shaking him and screaming, "Henry, Henry! Wake up! We need you! Henry! Henry!"

Gallant felt a prick as the needle penetrated his skin. A shot of adrenalin brought him sharply awake, and he tried to sit up, then fell back with a groan as pain seared across his temples. Pressing his hands to his head, he strained to find a mental picture of the battle. The attack depended on his leadership, but the image eluded him.

All he could see were swirling pictures of ships, UP and Titan, pitted against each other amid a hurricane of lightning and fury.

Panic tugged at Gallant's awareness. His mind was blank. He couldn't sense anything over the confusion that churned in his head.

As the flotilla maneuvered without specific orders, squadron commanders tried to coordinate their actions. But none of them had a comprehensive understanding of the entire battle scene.

The battle began to slip away from Gallant's grasp as Titan missiles continued to pound the UP fleet. With the squadrons forced to operate independently, the flotilla devolved into disarray.

"Henry! Henry!" Sam shouted again.

Gallant didn't respond. He wanted to run away. He wanted to hide.

He was afraid!

The fear was palpable. It consumed him. He was afraid he would fail the mission. He was afraid he would get his shipmates killed. He was afraid he would die. But most of all, he was afraid that Neumann was right all along.

He recalled Neumann's words during his Eagle qualification flight; "I know that when it counts, you'll let us down."

That thought swallowed him. He put his face into his hands and closed his eyes. He wanted it to all go away.

But it didn't go away. There was nowhere to run

or hide.

Gallant picked his head up and pushed down the fear.

He shook his head, trying to regain the clarity the AI gave him. Without it or the genetic enhancements of the other pilots, he had to find the strength within himself.

"I'm . . . OK. I'm OK," Gallant stammered through his disorientation.

I must get myself together. I'm costing lives.

He closed his eyes again, willing the dizziness to stabilize while he pulled his neural interface back into position.

"Commander Gallant! Gallant!" The communications system sputtered back to life. "What's happening there?"

Gallant pressed back into his seat just in time to see *Remarkable* explode in a massive fireball. He flinched, then gritted his teeth, determined to make up for his loss of control.

Restoring his mental control, he focused his mind on recognizing ships and their trajectories. Once more, he created a cohesive image of the battlefield.

"Sam, I'm on top of it again." He assigned priority targets, coordinated the squadrons, and ordered a second barrage from the bombers. With renewed precision, they launched their missiles at close range. The fighters had little trouble eliminating the insufficient Titan counterattack.

Jupiter Fleet concentrated its fire on damaged alien ships. Gallant coordinated the fighters' antimissile missiles. UP countermeasures proved effective at decoying the incoming Titan missiles.

But the battle was a costly one. Fighters and bombers were dropping out of formation, and escape pods were being released.

The Titan ships launched another missile barrage at the fighters. For several minutes, the UP ships were in turmoil, adjusting to the incoming missiles. Gallant coordinated the antimissile swarm to defend the formation. It was an effort for Gallant to think clearly. He could only compel his mind to it by an exertion of sheer will. He was tired and tense, but he had bought breathing space for the battlecruisers of Jupiter Fleet. They were limping off, out of range of the Titan forces, given new life.

Another volley from the Titans headed toward the flotilla bombers. Gallant spun the formation around, bringing their full antimissile salvo to cover the bombers.

The crossfire decimated the Titan defenses. One destroyer took a direct hit that shredded its armor, tearing a gaping hole in the side that scattered debris and vented its atmosphere. As more and more ships fell to the onslaught, the remaining Titan ships began to retreat from the battlefront. Leaving their crippled ships behind, they began streaming away from Jupiter Station toward the dark reaches of space. Gallant noticed with satisfaction that each ship looked to be operating independently. Their collective functioning had been disrupted, leaving the force spent and in disarray. The enemy was broken.

Gallant ignored the retreating Titan force. He concentrated on finishing off the crippled ships. Even before he could order another attack, however, the damaged ships self-destructed.

Meanwhile, the Marines showed their famous grit by counterattacking the Titan forces at Kendra. The long volcanic coastline on Ganymede revealed close combat action. Soon, Titan positions fell to the Marines.

The remaining Titan ground forces were hastily evacuated in their support ships. They headed out toward Saturn, leaving the asteroids and Jupiter frontier clear of operational enemy ships.

Only two ships, both badly damaged, remained from Jupiter Fleet. The aftermath meant rescuing the many wounded men and women stranded in escape pods drifting among the wrecked ships. He radioed *Repulse*, "Flotilla Commander Gallant reporting for rescue duty, sir."

Several days later, Admiral Collingsworth led Mars Fleet to Jupiter.

The liberation of the Jupiter frontier produced elation amongst the population. The Titan fleet had been driven off, back to the outer planets. Ganymede had been liberated from the alien ground forces. It should have been a time of unrestrained celebration. But no one was fooled into thinking the war was over. United Planets had won this round. There was time enough to worry about the next round later. For now, there was still the task of picking up the pieces in the aftermath of the conflict.

The battle for Jupiter left devastation and pain. A huge debris field of derelict ships remained in orbit. Colonists emerged from their bunkers to find shattered homes and to look for missing loved ones. Hospitals overflowed with injured bodies and traumatized victims. It would be necessary to resettle the colonists to resume a normal life. The hope was that they could re-establish their lives in a secure environment. But the threat, though turned aside for the moment, could rear its ugly head again at any moment.

PRIORITIES

29

A month after the rout of the Titans, a tiny shuttlecraft left Repulse, heading toward Jupiter Station. It maneuvered to avoid the worst of the solar radiation. Chatter about various ship movements and personnel transfers choked the communications channel. With an expert eye, the pilot navigated the brisk shuttlecraft traffic from the many warships, all on their way to Jupiter Station. Myriad trade ships from the Ganymede settlements only added to the congestion.

Gallant leaned forward in the copilot seat next to Jake, marveling at the region's transformation.

Jupiter's frontier is returning to normal.

Red sat behind him. Practically everyone on the frontier was attending the award ceremony on Jupiter Station.

"We'll dock in a few minutes; best to stay strapped in your seats," said Jake as he eased the ship toward the docking bay.

Raising his voice over the noise of the thrusters. Red said, "Did you know Kelsey arrived on a transport ship from Mars yesterday?"

Gallant tried to conceal a smile and failed. "Thanks."

Red said, "I've been to award ceremonies before, but with so many awards, decorations, and commendations, this one will be extraordinary. But, Henry, even with all those being honored, you'll be the show's star."

Lost in his thoughts, Gallant didn't hear.

Only when the spacecraft docked did he rouse himself from the reverie. Then, realizing that he had arrived a few minutes before the noon shuttle, Gallant walked past the auditorium. The preliminary formalities of the ceremony were beginning.

An orator was delivering opening comments. "Good morning, ladies, and gentlemen. Today, we honor members of the Space Force for their courage and dedication to protecting the frontier. We are pleased to have Governor Anderson of the Jupiter colonies presiding. We welcome family, friends, and colleagues of our award recipients. We are delighted you could join us in recognizing their contributions."

Gallant watched as Admiral Collingsworth stood stone-faced before the political leaders. Finally, the governor was introduced, and he began delivering a speech extolling the virtues of the fleet that drove off the Titans. The colonists applauded loudly and often.

Though the opening ceremony was underway,

the awards presentation wouldn't start for another hour. So, at noon, Gallant slipped out and returned to the passenger terminal to look for someone special.

Gallant saw Kelsey before she saw him and watched as she approached, a smile curving his lips. His vision shrank until she was the only one who existed in the crowded terminal. He drank in sight— the fashionable robin's-egg-blue outfit that matched her eyes. Her hazelnut hair was caught in a bun, highlighting her creamy complexion and warm smile.

He tugged at the collar of his newly tailored dress uniform. A single tangled lock of brown hair fell across his forehead, and he brushed it back with impatient fingers.

She caught sight of him and waved, quickening her pace. Gallant's demeanor didn't change, but his stomach lurched and flip-flopped. He stared, feeling the sweat on his palms as he clenched his fists, trying to steady their trembling. He had come specifically to meet Kelsey, yet now at the sight of her, his heart raced, and his vision blurred.

He flashed back to the memory of her body sprawled on the floor of the Eagle, her uniform torn and bloodied. He longed to reach out and pull her close, feel the warmth of her arms around him, reassure himself that she was real and whole. Instead, their past professional relationship had become filled with shared personal dangers. Still, he stood unmoving, hands at his side, afraid she would vanish the way she always did in his imagination.

He stood frozen, drinking her in, hoping she would speak first, but she didn't. As the mist slowly cleared his eyes, he tried to say something to ease the unbearable uncertainty. Finally, he stammered, "Are you well?"

Kelsey said, "Never better." She waited, her eyes probing his, and then added softly, "It's good to see you. I've missed you."

Have you missed me? I've missed you too. Gallant heard the words in his mind, but his mouth refused to say them.

Kelsey put her fingers to his lips as if they contained some extraordinary healing power that would give voice to his thoughts. The intimacy of the gesture released a deluge of emotions and impulses. But still, he hesitated, uncertain of her feelings. Then her fingers traced his jaw and trailed down the front of his uniform, and blind instinct took over.

He stepped forward and wrapped his arms around her. Their lips touched.

The moment shattered at the sound of a booming voice. "Gallant! Mitchel!"

They jumped apart as if shocked by lightning and turned to see Commander Eddington glaring at them.

"Here you are!" he said, panting. "I've looked everywhere. Gallant, the governor, wants to meet you before you receive your award. Come with me. Mitchel, why aren't you in uniform?"

He turned to walk away, then said over his shoulder, "Move it, you two. Besides the ceremony, we still must deal with the Titans. So, you need to get your priorities straight."

Gallant and Kelsey looked at each other. Then, with a glint of mischief in her eyes, Kelsey asked, "Just what are your priorities, Henry?"

Placing his hand under her chin, Gallant tilted her head and kissed her.

- the end. -

FROM THE AUTHOR:

I hope you enjoyed this book. I must confess —I'm proud of my characters and the story they tell. Henry is bold and brave, with a strong sense of duty—qualities I admire. Please post a review on Amazon: Midshipman Henry Gallant. Your feedback encourages me to work harder on the next book.

In gratitude,

H. Peter Alesso.

Book two is available:

LIEUTENANT HENRY GALLANT

In an era of genetic engineering, Lieutenant Henry Gallant is the fleet's only Natural (non-genetically enhanced) officer. Despite his superiors' concerns that he is not up to the challenge, his unique mental abilities have proven essential to the defense of the United Planets in its fight against the Titan invaders.

Serving on the first FTL prototype, the *Intrepid,* on its maiden voyage to Tau-Ceti, Gallant finds a lost human colony on the planet Elysium.

The colony's leader, Cyrus Wolfe, has allied himself with an ancient artificial intelligence That had lain dormant on the planet for millennia but is now willing to protect the colonists against the Titans.

Gallant allied himself with Alaina Hepburn, the leader of the democratic opposition. With Alaina's help, he discovers a sinister ulterior motive behind the AI's apparent helpfulness. He must match his exceptional mind against the complexity of machine intelligence to escape the ultimate trap and prevent the extermination of humanity.

In Lieutenant Henry Gallant, one man pits the naked human mind against the perspicacity of machine intelligence.

Click the *Follow* button on the author page to be notified of future books.

Amazon Author: H. Peter Alesso